"Who the hell you are?" Tis[...]

She kept her voice [...] people at the party. *[...] around!*

"You're not fit to drive home." Mitch was surprised at how much he cared about Tish's safety.

Tish was furious. "Well, listen, Mr. Law Enforcement Officer. Making wine is what I do for a living, and I do not drink past my capacity. Ever."

Tish turned to leave, but Mitch grabbed her arms and pulled her towards him. His kiss was impatient, angry. Yet his tongue's erotic dance sent hot shivers zigzagging up her spine.

With a gasp, she pushed Mitch away and stared at him wordlessly. She couldn't think of anything to say.

"See, what did I tell you?" he asked bleakly. "I'll take you home. Wait here."

Tish found a chair and collapsed onto it. Her knees wouldn't hold her any longer. Mitch Connor was right. Suddenly she didn't feel fit to drive.

And it wasn't because of the wine.

For Quincy Elizabeth

ACKNOWLEDGMENTS

Many thanks to Mert Baarts, Lieutenant Commander,
California Highway Patrol, for answering questions about
law enforcement with patience and good humor.
Thanks, also, to the staff of the Spokane Wine Company
for information about reduced alcohol wines.

———— ~ ————

KELLY STREET
is also the author
of this novel in
Temptation

ONLY HUMAN

Under Her Influence

KELLY STREET

MILLS & BOON LIMITED
ETON HOUSE, 18-24 PARADISE ROAD
RICHMOND, SURREY TW9 1SR

All the characters in this book have no existence outside the imagination of the Author, and have no relation whatsoever to anyone bearing the same name or names. They are not even distantly inspired by any individual known or unknown to the Author, and all the incidents are pure invention.

All rights reserved. The text of this publication or any part thereof may not be reproduced or transmitted in any form or by any means, electronic or mechanical, including photocopying, recording, storage in an information retrieval system, or otherwise, without the written permission of the publisher.

This book is sold subject to the condition that it shall not, by way of trade or otherwise, be lent, resold, hired out or otherwise circulated without the prior consent of the publisher in any form of binding or cover other than that in which it is published and without a similar condition including this condition being imposed on the subsequent purchaser.

First published in Great Britain in 1993 by Mills & Boon Limited, Eton House, 18-24 Paradise Road, Richmond, Surrey TW9 1SR

© Joy Tucker 1992

ISBN 0 263 78319 7

21 - 9306

Made and printed in Great Britain

1

THE WAIL OF A SIREN grew louder and louder.

Tish D'Angeli didn't hear it over the rattling of the engine. The glare of the sun shimmered over the dirt road, making potholes and bumps difficult to see. She concentrated on steering the dented subcompact as fast as she could over the treacherous surface. She tried not to think about the bald tires. A blowout would be disastrous out here in the middle of nowhere.

The hills she was driving past weren't *actually* nowhere. Fifteen years ago this undeveloped part of Sonoma County had been home, and she'd hated it. She, like most restless teenagers raised in the California backwater, had found farm life in the foothills of the Sierra Nevadas hopelessly monotonous.

So many years had passed. She had left before hordes of tourists descended on Sonoma and neighboring Napa Counties. before California wines began winning gold medals. Before the restaurants along the highway began catering to the upscale San Francisco crowd. A hungry woman couldn't even get a simple cheeseburger anymore.

Her stomach rumbled. She'd had a few pieces of pink roast duck and paper-thin vegetable slices for lunch. The whole thing had been delicious, artistically arranged, and skimpy. Right this minute she would have killed for a large, greasy burger with lots of mayo.

Tish started to worry. She was going to be late for her grandparents' fiftieth wedding anniversary, though she was sure this poorly maintained road led to the tiny chapel where the couple were to renew their vows. But the fields on either side had once been used for cattle grazing. Now, all she could see for miles were endless rows of grapevines. These dusty hills provided some of the best grape-growing conditions in the world. She should know; making wine was her business, even if her current job restricted her to the routine tasks of quality control for a major winery.

Tish gripped the wheel tighter as she bounced in her seat. The car hadn't been designed for rough terrain. It rattled over a cattle grid and the top of her head bumped against the low roof.

She muttered an unladylike curse and pressed her foot harder on the gas pedal. Death, or at least serious injury, was the only excuse her nice Nonna would accept if she showed up late for the ceremony. Her grandmother's temper was Italian clear through. The cool, stinging, Machiavellian type, not hot and excitable as Tish's had been before she'd learned to control it. *Once a D'Angeli, always a D'Angeli,* she thought with wry amusement, and no D'Angeli in her right mind would risk setting off Nonna's wrath.

Suddenly, her front tires sank into deep parallel ruts. The steering wheel jerked in her hands and spun out of control. The car bucked wildly. Terrified that the light car would somersault onto its nose if she braked too fast, she eased the brake down with anxious care. The noisy car shuddered to a halt in a cloud of dust.

Tish heard the shrieking of a police siren right behind her.

"WOULD YOU STEP OUT of the vehicle, ma'am?"

Mitch Connor was pleased that his voice sounded calm and official. It revealed nothing of the depth of his anger. He hated careless drivers. In ten years of police work, he'd seen too often how a car could become a destructive weapon in the hands of a drunk or a coked-up kid.

The woman opened her door, swung her legs out of the light blue vehicle and straightened. Mitch stepped back, abandoning the sideways stance he'd assumed before he'd rapped on her window just in case he had to confront a violent motorist. This young brunette seemed cooperative. She coughed a bit in the settling dust.

"Ma'am, will you please remove your dark glasses?"

She pulled them off. Mitch noted faint lines of stress or exhaustion at the corners of her brown, almond-shaped eyes. Her pupils reacted normally to the sunlight, not dilated or contracted by drugs.

"Name, please?"

"Tish D'Angeli."

The last name caught his attention. Her voice was clear and rather subdued—but that wasn't unusual for a traffic violator who'd been caught. She didn't appear intoxicated or dangerous. His anger began to recede and he relaxed slightly, assessing her. Her hair, brows and lashes weren't just brunette, they were raven's-wing black. An arched nose and superbly molded cheek-bones gave distinction to an oval face with full lips. Tish D'Angeli, demon driver, wasn't just pretty; she was beautiful. There were no rings on her left hand.

And her figure ... Mitch liked a woman who came equipped with something nice, something soft, to hold on to, and no one would ever mistake Ms. D'Angeli for a boy.

Her square shoulders and very full breasts weren't quite balanced by her slim hips. Some extra weight wouldn't have hurt her. Her calves were visible below an expensive-looking cream-colored skirt. They were just fine.

"May I see your license, please?"

Matching his careful, even tone, Tish replied, "It's in my purse." Slowly, without making any sudden moves that might give him an excuse to draw the gun in his holster, Tish reached back into the car.

A cop, she thought. Just her luck. The same kind of lousy, miserable, hellish luck that she'd hoped she'd finally put behind her.

She watched him as he inspected her license. Was there anything in the world scarier than a traffic cop? This one was tall—taller than she was—and in these heels she topped six feet.

"Do you know how fast you were going, Ms. D'Angeli?"

"About sixty miles per hour?" Tish guessed.

Aviator sunglasses with reflective silver lenses hid his eyes. He had a straight, thin nose and wore a sort of cowboy hat with a turned-up brim that shadowed his face. The combination should have looked silly. It didn't. It looked official. Intimidating.

He gave an impression of power. His beige uniform was sharply pressed. A chevron on his shoulder read, Sheriff's Dept. She glimpsed a bumper sticker on his unmarked car: To Serve And Protect.

Tish didn't think this particular cop was the type that would prove open to persuasion. Poker-faced and un-smiling, he looked to be all spit and polish. Altogether, he just didn't seem to be . . . amenable.

She glanced at her watch. Twelve-fifty. Aunt Aurelia had said one o'clock. There was no longer any doubt about Tish surviving this trip. Nonna was going to kill her.

"Uh, officer . . ."

Tish smiled tentatively.

Mitch turned her license over. Letizia Keller had been crossed out with a neat line on one side and Letizia D'Angeli typed in on the other. Divorced, probably. Widows rarely took back their maiden names. He looked up and caught the full effect of Tish's smile.

Momentarily he was dazzled. It was a standing joke in the department that Mitch was immune to women who used their wiles on him to get out of traffic tickets. A good cop was *supposed* to be immune, dammit. While on duty, anyway. But at twenty-nine years of age, five feet eleven, one hundred thirty pounds, Letizia D'Angeli of Cupertino, California, was definitely something special.

Not that her looks would make any difference in the way he treated her—while he was on duty.

Of course, he happened to be off duty.

Mitch cleared his throat. "Do you consider sixty miles per hour a safe speed on this kind of road?"

She turned on the smile again. "Safer than being late for my grandparents' anniversary. They're repeating their wedding vows in about—" she raised her arm so he could see her watch "—ten minutes. August and Magda D'Angeli. Do you know them?"

He wasn't about to admit that he did. The beautiful Ms. D'Angeli deserved to have the fear of God put in her for driving like a maniac. Perhaps he could at least scare her into having a healthy respect for her own safety.

"I'll ask the questions, Ms. D'Angeli," he said firmly.

Tish flushed. She didn't take well to patronizing males.

"Are you aware that this road has been abandoned by the county?" he continued.

"It doesn't seem to be in very good repair," she ventured.

"It's not," he agreed. "There's a bridge out about a quarter mile farther on."

"A bridge!" Tish tried to remember one and couldn't. "A bridge? Seriously?"

"A bridge," he confirmed. "And frankly, at the speed you were traveling in this, uh, vehicle . . ."

Mitch let his words trail off as he looked at her car. He hadn't even been accurate about the color, he thought with disgust. Her handprint on the dusty door showed up dark, not light blue. The body was crumpled with the scars of old accidents, and a wide scratch along the side was rusting.

The car didn't match the lady. If those pearl earrings were real, the demure pieces of jewelry would be worth a month's salary for a working stiff like him. She was probably wearing about a thousand bucks on her back. The lightweight suit shouted "designer." On the other hand, her transportation cried "rust bucket."

"I bought this car secondhand a couple of months ago," she burst out defensively. "It looked like this when I got it. The previous owner was a college student. Deputy, I don't usually drive like a madwoman. I've never even had a ticket before. And I know it sounds like a lie, but I honestly didn't hear your siren."

Smooth as syrup, Mitch said, "So you admit you were driving recklessly."

Her soft brown eyes opened wide. *At least she's beginning to realize this is serious*, he decided. She didn't panic, though; he'd give her credit for that.

"May I ask if you're planning to give me a ticket? If so, could you do it quickly, please?"

"Not so fast," he said mildly, pulling off his sunglasses and tucking them into his shirt pocket.

Nice enough looking man, Tish thought. His eyes were a lighter brown than hers, and hard. His mouth looked hard, too. His face was narrow with a good nose, strong jawline and definite cheekbones, sandy brows. His forehead was lined, as if his thirty-odd years of living hadn't been easy.

A hunter of humans. A spark of awareness skated up and down her spine. Tish told herself it was simply her survival instinct kicking in, recognizing a predator.

Mitch watched the flare of emotion in her eyes. Liking or dislike? He wanted to know. It had been a long time since he'd felt this kind of instant interest—attraction, curiosity, combined with a flicker of healthy lust.

He checked his wristwatch. Twelve fifty-five. Time to bring their little comedy to an end if either of them was going to be sufficiently on time to escape one of Nonna D'Angeli's scoldings. Due to the demands of his job, he'd been late to dinner at the D'Angeli house several times. He knew how the matriarch of the family regarded tardiness, and today's occasion was a special one. Even a marriage-burned skeptic like him could admit that. Ms. D'Angeli certainly wouldn't thank him if he caused her to be on the receiving end of Nonna's softly spoken wrath.

He handed her license back to her. "I won't be citing you, Ms. D'Angeli. But I'd like you to promise to drive more carefully in the future." He softened his tone deliberately. "I've seen a lot of accidents. Believe me, they aren't pretty."

"Thank you," she said hurriedly, replacing her license in her wallet. "I will. Drive carefully, I mean."

Mitch got into the sedan. Tish called out, "Wait a minute! Can you tell me how to find the old chapel that used to be out here?"

"Sure." Suddenly he flashed her a grin. "Just follow me. I'm late, too."

Tish expelled an exasperated breath and got behind the wheel. *Oh, for Pete's sake! A friend of Nonna and Pa's?* He must know how angry Nonna was going to be.

Couldn't he have taken a little less time to deliver his lecture?

She slammed her door.

2

THE COP MAINTAINED an infuriating twenty miles per hour and his sedan kicked up just enough dust to irritate Tish. One o'clock came and went as the two cars poked along. She seethed with impatience. Apparently the big bozo up ahead was determined to teach her a lesson and didn't care if they were disastrously late.

He slowed even more as he babied his car down a dry, shallow streambed next to a ruined bridge. Tish still didn't remember the bridge, although she recognized the rock-strewn hill to her left with its eucalyptus trees scattered like sentinels across the horizon. As she followed the cop out of the gully, she shuddered. All that remained of the weathered structure were a few posts ringed with weeds and some splintered boards hanging askew.

It was easy to imagine her car crumpled over the wicked points of the pilings. *Damn.* The cop probably *had* saved her life. She ought to thank him. She mulled over that unpleasant reality until he signaled a turn into an open lot. They'd reached their destination.

Tish pulled into a parking space next to the sedan, switched off the engine and rubbed her damp palms on her skirt. She'd made it. Several times during the past hour, she'd doubted that she would.

She shook the collar of her thin blouse and shrugged her shoulders to loosen the fabric where it was sticking to her back. Perhaps she shouldn't have worn a suit. She'd planned on a long hot drive, but even comfortable raw silk had its limits.

Tish took her time. She was going to catch hell from the family anyway, and it was important to look well groomed, in control and unaffected by her divorce. Five more minutes really wouldn't make a difference. She freshened her coral lipstick and dabbed on more perfume.

Mitch walked around to Tish's door, his black leather boots crunching on the gravel surface. The sight of Tish fussing with her makeup gave his natural optimism a boost. She was going through the whole funny primping routine every woman seemed to find essential before she faced a man she found attractive—touching her hair, licking her lips, turning her chin to study her reflection in the rearview mirror.

He pulled open her car door.

"You look fine," he said. "And you smell wonderful."

Tish started. She hadn't actually forgotten her unwanted escort while she prepared to face her relatives. He wasn't the sort of man a woman found easy to forget, but his abrupt change of attitude amazed her. What had happened to Deputy By-the-Book?

If he could be informal, so could she. She gave him the kind of look she used to give her cousins when they were all outspoken teenagers. "Isn't that an awfully personal thing for a law officer to say?" she demanded, stepping out of the car.

"Yeah," he admitted cheerfully. "Ready to go in? We don't want to be late, do we?"

Tish was annoyed by his breezy manipulation. This overgrown, overbearing cop was more endurable when he was all spit and polish. "You know, my ex-husband was a lot like you."

"I'm glad we're talking about an *ex*-husband."

"Don't be. It wasn't a compliment."

"Ah. Not one of the good guys."

"I don't separate the world into good guys and bad guys," she retorted with a spurt of desperation. His behavior kept throwing her off balance. First he acted stern, then avuncular; now, was he coming on to her? She didn't need this kind of aggravation, not when she had to present a serene facade to her loving family.

"You don't? Then I have a chance, right?"

She looked up at his question. Did he mean to be crude, or funny, or kind?

He didn't give her the opportunity to ask. "You really don't have to rush in." He added blandly, "You didn't think this dog-and-pony show was going to start on time, did you? With your Aunt Aurelia in charge?"

Tish picked her way across the lot in her heels. He seemed to know the D'Angelis better than she did after eleven years away from home. And he had a really detestable habit of insisting on having the last word.

"I feel sorry for your wife. Or girlfriend." Two could play this sparring game.

He spoke abruptly. "You don't need to. I haven't got either at the moment."

She glanced up at him, surprised. "Really?" She'd simply assumed he had one or the other. Or possibly both. Walking beside him, she felt the impact of his virility. He had a natural authority, an easy self-confidence so instinctual she wondered if he was even aware of it. The sniping nature of their conversation didn't bother him; he seemed to be enjoying it. How odd. So was she. It wasn't her usual style of interaction. In fact, she'd avoided social situations over the past year. Her life had become gloriously private.

Which was just the way she'd liked it since she'd walked away from Jonathan Keller, his mansion, his world-famous gun collection and his yacht twelve months ago. Incredibly, it had taken her seven years to discover that the yacht's hot tub had come equipped with secretaries. In the plural, and in the nude.

That didn't mean she now believed that all men were unfaithful, but her ex-husband had left her with a mistrust of domineering men.

Not that many men produced sensual signals as strong as this deputy did. His uniform might be conservatively cut, but the pants outlined muscular thighs. He took off his hat, revealing neatly-cropped sandy hair. His short-sleeved shirt, crisp despite the wilting heat, exposed tanned, athletic arms with blond hair that glistened in the sunlight. He didn't swing his arms loosely when he walked; he held them flexed close to his body, ready for action. Just the way he moved advertised his masculinity.

Don't even think about it, Tish, she cautioned herself uncomfortably. *This is not some safe, wimpy type. And you don't need complications.*

"Look," she said as they approached the side door of the chapel, "at least this is exactly the way I remember it."

The building was surrounded by overgrown quince, the bell tower had no bell, the frame exterior needed paint. She paused in the doorway. The plaster interior still lacked electric lighting. Rosy beams of light filtered through the stained glass and wavered over the people inside. None of the windows matched and Tish realized for the first time they must have been scavenged from other churches that were being remodeled or torn down.

She took a deep breath. The place smelled the same— of beeswax candles and of sulphur from hundreds of burned matches.

It smelled like childhood.

The cop was studying her. "Used to come here a lot?"

"All the time. It wasn't closed up when I was a kid. Every Sunday I sat between Nonna and Pa, second row on the right. The only reason I didn't get married here was because my in-laws claimed it gave them a cramp in the soul." *Naturally it would,* she thought. The chapel was too poor for their tastes.

This wasn't the moment to be brooding about the over-and-done-with. Besides, the deputy was murmuring, "See? What did I tell you? The ceremony hasn't started yet."

Glancing toward the rear, Tish glimpsed ivory crepe de chine near the vestibule. With a wheeze, a march began, played on the badly out-of-tune organ.

Her cousin, Belle, beckoned furiously from the third row. A large, firm hand on Tish's back nudged her for-

ward and she slid into place next to Belle. With eight
people, the short pew was now quite full. The cop ignored that fact and pushed in beside Tish. She decided
that sensitivity was not one of his outstanding char-
acteristics.

The others in the row craned their necks to see who
was trying to make room where any idiot could see that
none existed. After the deputy had been thoroughly
inspected, they began shifting over to make space for
him. Whether they knew him or were simply accommodating his size or his uniform or his sheer force of
personality, Tish couldn't tell. He squeezed onto the
seat beside her.

Obscurely embarrassed—after all, his manners or
lack of them weren't her responsibility—Tish stood as
her grandmother began a stately walk up the aisle.

"Looks great, doesn't she?" the cop murmured appreciatively.

Tish nodded without turning around. "She looks
wonderful," she whispered.

Nonna was wearing the gown she'd worn on her
wedding day, fifty years before. Tish recognized it from
old photographs. Faded snapshots hadn't reproduced
the crepe's sheen, now subtly darkened to gold with the
patina of time, or done justice to the severe beauty of
its slim, early-twenties styling. The dress had been in
the family since Nonna's mother became a bride.

Nonna's firmly corseted figure revealed the lovely
lines Tish inherited. Most of Nonna's sixty-nine years
had been spent in the harsh California sun, but her
wrinkles did not conceal the radiance of her smile. With
a shock, Tish realized that Nonna's hair, swept up un-

der the antique lace veil, had turned pure white. Eighteen months before, her hair had been iron gray streaked with black.

Tish had always thought Nonna's extraordinary eyes were like a black sky filled with stars. They hadn't faded. Nor had Nonna's single-minded concentration. Her gaze was fixed on the short, stout man waiting at the altar.

None of his children or grandchildren had ever called August D'Angeli anything but Pa. His round face was red with emotion and pride. He wasn't exactly a romantic figure, but Tish blinked against a rush of tears. This was how love was supposed to be—something tangible, growing and deepening over the years, widening to envelop family and friends, exalting everyone fortunate enough to be touched by it.

Mitch noticed that the woman beside him was crying soundlessly. Not misting up, but really crying, tears streaming down her cheeks. Her breathing was controlled, her shoulders rigid. Ms. D'Angeli obviously didn't want anyone to notice her unhappiness. He couldn't fault her for it. He knew a little about that kind of pride.

Just as obviously, he couldn't let her go on. Her crying jag was gaining a momentum of its own, and her back and shoulders, angled into his chest by the tight fit in the pew, shuddered sporadically.

Tish realized dimly that the tears weren't going to stop. They had nothing to do with Jonathan. She'd already wept all the tears she intended to waste on him a long time ago. Maybe these were for herself. At any

rate, she was about to break into loud, humiliating sobs
and ruin Nonna and Pa's big day.

Just then, the man beside her wrapped one arm
comfortingly around her. Somehow his hand settled on
her waist, exactly where she was most sensitive and
vulnerable. The shock of being touched there at all
stopped the tears as effectively as if he had shut off a
faucet.

"It's all right," he whispered, his lips tickling her ear.
"Everything's fine. Okay now?"

"Okay."

"Good."

Tish drew a shaky breath as Nonna joined Pa at the
altar. They helped each other onto kneelers garlanded
with flowers. The deputy pulled Tish back and down
onto the seat before the rest of the congregation sat, so
she was able to grab her purse and begin hasty repairs.

Not even Belle seemed to think it strange that Tish
should be wiping mascara off her cheeks and discreetly blowing her nose. In fact, a good many tissues
and handkerchiefs were in play in the chapel. Tish's
moment of weakness over, she gradually relaxed, especially when the cop quietly moved his arm from
around her waist. Tish told herself it wasn't a big deal
that he immediately slid it along the backrest behind her
shoulders. The pew was just crowded.

The ancient words Nonna and Pa repeated were
beautiful. *For better or for worse. For richer or for
poorer. To have and to hold, cleaving only unto you.*

Babies cried and were hushed. The air in the little
church warmed with the heat of so many bodies packed
together on a summer day. The organ sounded truly

awful. It had all the melodious sweetness of a bagpipe smothering to death.

Tish remained acutely conscious of the man next to her. The humidity released the spiciness of his after-shave. Their thighs were pressed against each other. The casual pressure somehow felt . . . important. It provided her with the simple comfort of a man's mus-cled leg braced against her own—the way things were supposed to be, a natural consequence of *cleaving*, a blessing in a blessed place.

But she shouldn't be feeling this here and now with a stranger, however sexy he might be. The solidity and the comfort weren't really about sex, anyway.

Nonna and Pa stood, rather creakily, to face the guests. The congregation burst into applause.

The din drowned out even the organ. Tish jumped up and clapped till her palms stung as her grandpar-ents walked down the aisle, beaming at each other.

Picking up her purse, Tish stepped out of the pew, intending to follow the deputy. He had already disap-peared.

"Move, Tish," said Belle, busily pushing past her. "Long time no see. You coming to the reception?"

"Of course. But I need to give Nonna and Pa a hug first."

"Good luck." She nodded toward the rear of the chapel. "Everybody and his uncle is back there. They'll be kissing and slapping each other on the back forever. You might as well wait and see them at the party."

"I think I'd better see them now." Tish bit her lip.

Belle raised her eyebrows. "What's the matter? Not anxious for a cozy chat with Nonna?"

"I'm here to visit for two weeks." She couldn't keep a defensive note out of her voice. "It's just, well, you know how she is."

"Don't I just," Belle affirmed with feeling. "They could have used her in the Inquisition."

At Belle's ready sympathy Tish relaxed and smiled. "How does she do it? No torture chambers required. Just a cup of tea, a few slices of pantone bread, some sharply honed questions—"

"And no secret is safe from her. She's a pro."

The effectiveness of Nonna's methods of interrogation was one of the reasons Tish had stayed in Cupertino. She'd never been any good at concealment. In the aftermath of the divorce, she had needed time and distance to hide from Nonna's lively curiosity. Tish had finally achieved enough to face the family again. A job, an apartment, a new life.

Belle grimaced, creasing her heavy makeup. "Well, good luck. Mom wants me to baby-sit a couple of the older folks till we get to the hall. See you later. God, you look fabulous."

Belle clapped a hand to her mouth and glanced quickly around the chapel to see if anyone else had heard her swear in church. She waved at Tish with a wry, shamefaced grin, then plunged into the crowd.

Tish maneuvered as close to her grandparents as she could and saw Nonna's mouth shape her name. Tish nodded emphatically, relieved that she'd been noticed. Nonna blew her a kiss and waved her away before turning to another well-wisher.

Tish went back to her car and joined the lineup to exit the lot. Unscrambling the dozens of vehicles parked in

disarray looked like a mammoth undertaking to her.
But as she drove out, Tish saw the deputy directing the
snarled cars with the élan of a symphony conductor.
Arms waving, giving crisp signals, he looked toward
her.

Tish raised a hand in cheeky salute. He might have
seen her—she wasn't sure because of his sunglasses.

Tish turned on to the newly paved county road and
headed toward the hall where the reception would be
held. She maintained a sedate forty-five miles an hour
all the way.

3

THE FRATERNAL HALL was a perfectly awful cinder-block structure that had been tossed together in the fifties. The place was so utterly hideous, it took on a kind of charm. It had a flat roof and few windows. Outside and in, it was painted that apple-green shade used by institutions to encourage visitors to leave as soon as possible.

Tish knew the family could easily have afforded the country club for the reception. Certainly her grandparents owned enough valuable land to be considered moderately wealthy. It hadn't always been that way. For a long time, Pa and Nonna had struggled to make ends meet, selling their grapes. Those early years had left their mark. Pa and Nonna weren't cheap, exactly, but neither of them would feel comfortable in the upscale atmosphere of a club. They preferred the unpretentious, familiar hall.

A blast of cool air hit Tish as she pushed open the back door of the kitchen.

Ladies wearing big white aprons over flowered dresses bustled around.

"Letizia! My land, girl, how long has it been?"

"Too long, Mrs. Souza. How are you?"

"Not bad, not bad, barring a little female trouble."

All of the women were elderly acquaintances of her grandparents who knew Nonna or Pa slightly from church or the lodge or garden club. They hadn't attended the ceremony.

"You want to help? You'll need an apron. That's right, spread the cream cheese nice and thick, and don't be stingy with those slivered almonds. Of course, take a bite! Food's here to be eaten. Oh, Hazel, the bunions aren't the worst of it...."

Tish worked and nibbled as the ladies gossiped about their health with ghoulish matter-of-factness. Tish heard about hernias and slipped disks and how much better sex could be after the change-of-life. There was a dearth of easy chatter in her own life. The only voices she ever heard in the apartment came from the television set.

She peeked into the main room. A noisy throng was gathering around the linen-covered tables. She heard corks pop and glasses tinkle. The guests were getting impatient to celebrate in earnest.

She was ready to mingle, Tish told herself, but she needed these last few minutes of breathing space before she went out to brave all the love and understanding and pity waiting for her in the next room.

"Divorced" was bad enough. "Divorced and broke" was humiliating.

Technically, she couldn't be called broke at all. Her savings account was healthy with the settlement her lawyer had harangued out of her ex-husband and his lawyer. Despite her distaste for the whole process of suit and countersuit, she'd fought for what she believed she'd earned in her years of working, without credit, as a consultant to Jonathan's small wine-making operation. It was his toy, a little dream of a hobbyist's winery—the sort of trendy investment young millionaires liked to give themselves as treats. In the dust-and-ashes boredom of her existence as a society wife, it had been her life. She'd loved the challenge of using her rigorous college training, the joy of creating something special.

She meant to experience the challenge and the joy again. And every penny she could save, including the divorce settlement, would someday be the down payment on her dream: her own winery.

Cousin Belle bustled into the kitchen.

"There you are! The grands are fretting for you. Oh, leave the trays. Somebody will take care of them...."

Tish barely had time to strip off the apron before Belle yanked her into the thick of the crowd. Several guests called their names. A rounded goblet filled with red wine appeared in her hand. She took a quick swallow and then Pa barreled toward her, shouting, "Mia bambina!" in his cracked, hoarse bellow.

A second-generation immigrant and proud of it, Pa only used his Italian when he was deeply moved. Well, so was she. She pressed smacking kisses on his cheeks and got two in return.

"Too long! Too long! She's been away from us too long, huh?" He looked around for confirmation from the group of buddies who followed him and formed a sort of backdrop to his explosive energy.

His friends were all of his generation, dressed in their Sunday best and clutching brimming glasses. They nodded solemnly.

Tish laughed and spoke to the ones she recognized. "Mr. Fontana, I'm so glad to see you. How's the body-shop business? And Mr. Arata, you haven't changed one bit...."

They all blushed and preened and told her how pretty she looked and what a handful she used to be in days gone by. Some of the tight, tensed-up feeling in her chest evaporated. What had she been afraid of? These old darlings weren't going to dismiss her because she wasn't a rich man's wife anymore. They were simply and flatteringly happy to see her.

It was rather nice to be greeted by people who were happy to see her.

After a while Pa's friends' reminiscences began to repeat, so Tish held up her empty glass as an excuse to inch away. Wine never had much effect on her but she knew it would be foolish not to send some more food to her stomach to keep the heavy Zinfandel company.

Not everyone had the exquisite tact of Pa's cronies, of course. Belle caught up to her beside the prosciutto and melon balls, and asked the time. Tish pushed back the sleeve of her jacket and Belle promptly began to undermine Tish's self-possession.

"Your watch!" she exclaimed, staring at the cheap digital on Tish's wrist. "What happened to your platinum wristwatch? All those diamonds!"

Tish flinched. The gem-encrusted timepiece had come in handy. After a minimum of haggling, a jeweler had given her enough to pay her first and last months' rent on the small, horrendously expensive apartment that had been the best she could manage in Cupertino. There'd been enough left over to cover the security deposit and a week's worth of groceries. She hadn't been as lucky with the engagement ring. The proceeds from that had barely covered the second-hand car. She couldn't bring herself to sell her wedding band. She'd mailed it to her former mother-in-law.

The explanation hovered on the tip of her tongue. Then she licked her dry lips instead. Belle had always been good company but she did suffer from a compulsion to gossip. A hint of financial trouble and every D'Angeli on the continent would be informed that Tish, who'd been married to the millionaire, had some grandiose and crack-brained idea of turning herself into a *Falcon Crest* Jane Wyman.

As coolly as she could, Tish said, "I don't want to wear the watch anymore."

"Don't want— Oh, you mean because it was a present from Jonathan? That jerk. I don't blame you." Belle looked her over. "Your clothes are gorgeous. And you haven't put on an ounce. I could kill you. Every time I have a fight with Frank, I gain five pounds. What's your secret?"

"Yogurt," she answered truthfully. Belle didn't have to know Tish bought it because it was the least expensive form of protein. Or that in the months after Jonathan had cleaned out their joint bank account and before the settlement had come through, before she'd found a job, there had been days when she'd had blueberry yogurt for breakfast, lemon yogurt for lunch and vanilla yogurt for dinner.

The thought made her turn yearningly toward the buffet. Those little sausages looked awfully good.

Picking up her glass, which was mysteriously full once more, Tish wandered up and down the tables, sampling as she went.

Belle trailed after her, providing updates on each of the guests.

"There's Mrs. Gabrielli. For heaven's sake, stay away from her. She'll talk your ear off about her son. He's *still* in college and she wants him to marry money."

If she only knew, Tish thought with amusement.

"And Kathy— Remember her from school? She's into health foods. Her husband made her go in for surgery but she swears that cranberry juice got rid of her kidney stones."

Kathy's goblet was filled with a ruby liquid. Tish decided to be charitable. What the heck, maybe the woman *was* drinking cranberry juice.

"Oho. Look out. Tommy DeCarlo's seen you."

Tish smiled at her old classmate. "Hello, Tommy."

"Tish, I can't believe it!" Tommy's blond locks still fell boyishly over his forehead. To Tish they looked carefully styled. "You look more beautiful now than you did the night we went to the prom."

She shook her head at him. "It's nice of you to say so. A few years have passed since high school. You're looking pretty good yourself. What kind of work do you do?"

"Oh, you know. I close a deal now and then. Real estate."

Not too surprising, she thought. Tommy'd always had more than his fair share of charm. Selling would be a natural career for him to choose. She made a non-committal sound.

He apparently took it for encouragement. "Hey, want to find out if that magic is still there? Dance with me later, okay?"

Tish couldn't recall any magic. They'd dated regularly but not exclusively during high school. Maybe Tommy had manufactured different memories out of the PG-rated movies and sedate dances they'd attended together. This could get sticky. She hesitated. "Well..."

"Oh, come on. Take a chance." He smiled winningly.

She capitulated. "Sure. Thanks."

Tommy moved away to zero in on the smoked oysters at another table. Belle grinned. "He's quite a catch, they say. Got that lifeguard kind of bod. Still surfs, can you believe it? And he's making a bundle with his business, the way land values have inflated around here. You won't do much better if you're looking."

"I'm not looking."

"Loosen up," Belle advised. "Nothing wrong with keeping your eye out. Tommy's about it as far as men under sixty are concerned, except for Mitch Connor. And you already know him."

Tish caught Belle's speculative glance. She was sure she didn't know anybody named Mitch. "No. Should I?"

"I should say so. You were almost sitting on his lap at the chapel. How come you always have the luck?"

Tish could think of another word for it. "Oh, him. A little too much machismo for my taste," she muttered through a cheese straw.

"You think so? I think he's sexy. But then, so is Frank." Belle giggled. "Better yet, Frank says I'm sexy, too."

The nature of Frank's attraction to Belle had never been in doubt, even in high school with teachers on guard seven hours a day and Aunt Aurelia doing sentry duty the other seventeen. And no wonder, thought Tish. A long jaw and an overbite conspired to add a horsey quality to her cousin's allotment of the family's classic features, but bearing four children had only embellished her eye-catching shape with a certain lushness. Today, Belle was wearing a bright floral dress and a strong dose of drugstore perfume.

"You look really nice, Belle," Tish said gently. "Frank has a lot to be grateful for."

"You bet he does. I tell him all the time."

Tish sipped her wine. A couple of glassfuls and the flavor didn't drag on her palate as much as it had at first, although Zinfandel grapes were very strong. Still, she wrinkled her nose at its harsh bouquet. The aroma was doing combat with the stinging florals of Belle's scent. Tish's highly developed senses of taste and smell counted as assets in the creation of fine wine, but in ordinary situations they had their drawbacks.

Everyone else drank with obvious enjoyment. None of the others, as far as she knew, made a living as a wine maker. The people here grew grapes aplenty to sell to any of a hundred vintners in the state, just as the D'Angelis did, but a vineyard was as different from a winery as a cattle ranch from a shoe factory.

Belle poked Tish's arm. "There he is. Mitch Connor. Sure you don't want me to introduce you?"

"No, thanks," Tish replied dryly. "We sort of met when he pulled me over on the old Souza road for driving too fast."

"He what?"

"Honestly. Siren, flashing lights, the whole bit. I guess I'm lucky. He didn't give me a ticket, just a very stuffy warning."

"Tish, where are your brains? You're supposed to be the smart cousin. Mitch couldn't ticket you on a private road. I've heard he's death on reckless driving, though. It's understandable."

"Understandable?" Tish repeated automatically. She shouldn't be feeling angry. The deputy had saved her from what might have been a nasty accident out on the deserted road, yet it had taken a certain amount of cruelty to let her believe he could give her a ticket. Resentment stirred.

"Yeah. Five, six years ago, before he showed up in Sonoma County, his wife got killed in a car crash. She was pregnant, no other kids. He took it real hard. Quit the highway patrol, came up here looking for a change."

The tan hat swiveled as he turned his head toward them and a pair of fox-brown eyes met hers. Although Tish knew he couldn't hear Belle's voice over the nearly rock-concert volume of conversation in the room, she felt intense embarrassment. Somehow she sensed a man like him would want his private hurts buried, safe from the kindly prying of his neighbors.

She dropped her gaze to the scarlet toenails revealed by Belle's sandals. As far as she was concerned, intuition didn't exist. Especially not in herself. The divorce provided pretty conclusive proof she shouldn't go around making snap judgments about men.

So why did she suddenly feel positive that Mitch Connor hid genuine sensitivity behind his so-tough official act and the quick flash of his grin? She owed him a thank-you. Fine. Sometime in the next two weeks she would give him a call or write him a note. She'd find a way to express her gratitude that didn't involve hormones or sympathy or any other such messy human reactions.

Belle continued her inexhaustible chatter. Finally she paused and regarded Tish with raised eyebrows. Her last remark obviously required an answer. Quickly Tish said, "I haven't spoken to Nonna yet. Catch you later, all right?"

Nonna was holding court from a brocade chair near the stage. Tish leaned over to kiss her.

"Everything is lovely, Nonna. Congratulations."

"Felicitations," her grandmother corrected. "Congratulations are for the groom. He's thrilled so many of the family could be here."

The indulgent comment, delivered in Nonna's most winsome voice, couldn't possibly have been taken for a criticism—unless one happened to have spent all one's teenage years growing up around Nonna.

"I'm here now," Tish pointed out softly. "But I've been a rat lately, haven't I?"

"You will never hear me say so, Letizia."

"It's true, though. I needed to—to put myself back together, that's all. I'm sorry I haven't been to see you since the divorce." Tish reached out tentatively and rearranged a fold of the fragile lace veil. Her fingertips brushed the soft white hair. Old business needed to be aired. "You've always been good to me, ever since Mama and Daddy died. You never complained once about taking on a fourteen-year-old monster when you and Pa ought to have been planning for your retirement."

The wrinkles around Nonna's mouth puckered briefly. "Why should we complain about the joy of our old age? You were never a monster, dearest, just so very unhappy."

"I was awful. If you liked the blue dress, I bought the green one. If you wanted me to date Rick, I went out with Tom. How could you stand me?"

"Love puts up with all kinds of things." Nonna patted her hand. "It's amazing. Let me look at you. Talking on the phone is not the same—all that expensive long-distance . . ."

Mitch watched granddaughter and grandmother from across the room. No detective ability was required to see where Ms. D'Angeli got her looks.

Did Tish have the same combination of mental toughness and overflowing heart that had drawn him into friendship with Nonna? His own mother had never been a wellspring of maternal affection. Nonna D'Angeli had provided some of the mothering he'd missed in childhood. Not that he wanted to inspire maternal feelings in Tish.

He swallowed the last of his cola and grimaced. He'd been nursing the stuff for the better part of an hour. By now it had gone flat and consequently tasted far too sweet. A cracker spread with salmon pâté effectively killed the flavor. He was eyeing another cracker when

his toe struck a small, round object that had rolled under the buffet table.

A pearl earring.

It certainly looked like one of Tish's—a large pearl
on a gold post. He picked it up and revised his estimate
of its worth sharply downward. The little globe
couldn't be real, or even cultured. Up close, its milky
surface lacked the elusive depth it ought to have had.
The thing was no more than a plastic bead glued to a
base-metal stud.

Still, the lady might like to have it back. And it provided a legitimate reason for him to seek her out. Mitch
had never been shy around women, but he'd wanted to
give her a chance to greet her relatives before he reminded her that he was around. It was almost time for
him to report to work. If he intended to make a move,
it had to be soon.

Tish's long slim fingers were enfolded in Nonna's
gnarled brown ones as Nonna spoke softly in her flow-
ing voice. Mitch couldn't make out the words. Nonna's voice was like that. It occurred to him—not for the
first time—that it was a damned seductive voice for a
woman celebrating her fiftieth wedding anniversary.
Tish's voice was slightly higher-pitched, but it had the
same bone-stirring, honeyed quality.

Both women looked up as he approached. Abruptly
he became conscious of his size-twelve feet and his
freckled hands that were approximately twice the size
of theirs. The one social skill cops were taught was how
to barge into any situation without revealing awk-
wardness, so he said, "Nonna, you're the prettiest bride
I've ever seen," and held out the earring.

Tish stared at his palm. She was more aware of its size and its calluses than of the bauble it cupped so delicately until Nonna asked sweetly, "Is it yours, dearest?"

Her fingers flew to her earlobes. "Oh. Oh, yes, I guess it is. Thanks. I must have lost the little screw thing."

Calmly Nonna picked it out of Mitch's hand and inspected it before she passed it to Tish. "Best put them both in your purse, Letizia."

Tish took the other earring off and tucked them into her narrow alligator bag.

A middle-aged man strode onto the stage and squeezed a chord out of a large accordion.

Nonna leaned forward, preparing to rise from her chair. She accepted Mitch's swiftly offered hand under her elbow. "Now, that's enough," she scolded as soon as she was standing, pulling her arm away and giving him a bright smile. "I do fine once I'm up and moving. Gus will be looking for me for the first waltz. When everybody joins in, Mitch, I want you to dance with Letizia. She's been such a stranger lately. Nobody's asked her."

"Nonna!" gasped Tish.

Her grandmother evaded Tish's indignation by slipping into the crowd. Brown eyes met. "That was pretty transparent, I'm afraid," Tish said.

"I would have asked you to dance anyway," Mitch assured her, "but this is better." At her puzzled glance, he added, "No suspense. I assume you're just as scared of Nonna D'Angeli as the rest of us mortals. So now I don't have to worry about you turning me down. You wouldn't dare."

"You can't fool me. You're not scared or worried about anything." Surprise rippled through Tish. "Sorry, I don't usually say things like that."

"Like what?"

"Personal things." She swirled the ruby wine in her glass. "Listen, you don't have to dance with me. This place is packed with cousins and guys I went to high school with and little old men who remember me in braces. In fact, I've already been asked to dance. There's no reason for you to feel obligated."

"Please. Give me a break. Next you'll say you can cut a rug with your Aunt Aurelia."

She took a sip. The stuff really wasn't as bad as she'd thought. "No, I won't say that. If you're sure."

He frowned at her glass but said mildly, "I'm sure. You know, I can't get over how much you look like your grandmother. I didn't see it right away but the resemblance is uncanny. Like a negative, a reversed image. The features are the same, only your hair's black and hers is white. Your skin is pale and hers is tanned."

"Sun," Tish commented. "Nobody knew about the dangers of too much sun when Nonna was young. Anyway, she didn't have any choice. She worked out in the vines like any field hand while she and Pa were getting the vineyard established."

"Quite a woman."

"Yes."

"Your eyes aren't as dark as hers. I can't see any resemblance to Gus."

Tish tried to look severe but her eyes danced. "Better watch it. Pa wouldn't like to hear that at all."

Mitch grinned back. "Let's face it, though, it's just as well. Nonna's got the good looks."

"Pa has a beautiful soul," Tish defended quickly.

Mitch gave her a straight look. "I know. Your grandparents have been very good to me. It means something to be treated like family."

Maybe she liked him better without the granite facade, after all. "I owe you a thank-you for the warning about the bridge. If you hadn't come along—"

"Here comes the big moment," he interrupted. "Ready?"

The beaming accordion player launched into an arrangement of "The Anniversary Waltz," heavy on the oom-pah-pahs. The guests backed away to clear a space. Pa led Nonna in widening circles and swung her in a smooth arc to enthusiastic applause. He danced surprisingly well.

Tish's aunts and uncles, then her cousins and their spouses joined in. Finally Mitch took the glass out of Tish's hand, set it down and drew her to the center of the floor.

"I hope you don't mind," he said, liking the feel of her in his arms. She fit him just right, her eyes a fraction lower than his. Her pliant body responded to each movement he made, swaying to the music with natural grace.

"Mind?"

"Yeah. I can't keep up with these youngsters bouncing around in here. Mind if we dance slow?"

"Oh." The accordion player pounded out the song as if it were one of the rowdier polkas. In contrast, the rhythm Mitch set was definitely, wickedly slow. Hip occasionally brushed hip, and chest touched chest in light grazes that left Tish's breasts tingling in anticipation of the next fleeting contact. "No, I don't mind."

"Good." He pulled her closer.

Tish was surprised at her heightened awareness. The sensitive zone around her waist tingled with pleasure. She'd only met the man this afternoon. Comforting concern had been the watchword in the chapel. Now when their thighs met and pressed together, warmth stole between her legs. The soft, hot ache was part of the wine, the heavy beat of the music, the man who held her close, the brown eyes that seemed to wait for her at lovemaking distance.

For heaven's sake, she thought, *you aren't even sure you like him*.

The waltz ended in a clash of discordant chords. They stopped moving but Mitch retained his distracting embrace.

Tish gave him a strained smile. "I think I'll have another glass of wine. If you'll excuse me—"

"No."

"I— What?"

"No, I won't excuse you," he said in such a pleasant tone that Tish couldn't believe she'd heard him correctly. "No more wine for you. Not if you're driving."

"I beg your pardon, but who the hell do you think you are?"

"For one thing, I'm a law-enforcement officer. For another, I'm the guy who saw you putting away about twenty ounces of wine in a one-hour period. Are you planning to drive back to Cupertino today?"

"I'm staying with my grandparents for a couple of weeks. Not that it's any of your business. Do you think I'm *drunk?*"

"You don't exhibit the classic symptoms," he admitted. "But I'm willing to bet your blood alcohol is way over the legal limit."

"Well, listen, Mr. Law-Enforcement Officer. Making wine is what I do for a living and I am perfectly aware of how it alters sensory and motor control. I don't drink past my capacity. Ever. Some indifferent Zinfandel isn't going to put me under the table. I have a hyper metabolism."

"You have a hyper mouth, that's for sure," Mitch muttered.

Tish was furious, but before she could say anything else, Mitch pressed a hard, dry kiss to her lips. It was impatient, angry. Not like a kiss should be. Yet beneath the anger Tish sensed concern. She wouldn't respond to his arrogance but his concern kept her from jerking away. Stubbornly she kept her lips closed.

Mitch lifted his head. His harsh breath warmed her ear and the imprint of his mouth lingered. Tish gulped and stared at him with wide eyes. Very gently, he cupped her chin in his hands. His face was expressionless—except for the analytical glitter in his eyes. The contradiction between his caring hands and cold gaze confused her. Her knees were about to crumple and she couldn't have spoken even if she'd been able to think of something to say.

"See? What did I tell you?" he asked bleakly. "You're not fit to drive home. I'll take you. Wait here."

Tish found a chair and collapsed into it. Mitch Connor happened to be right. Suddenly she didn't feel fit to drive.

But not because of the wine.

4

"HOW ABOUT THAT DANCE?"

Tommy DeCarlo beamed at her. Shock still blanking out coherent thought, Tish let Tommy pull her to her feet and lead her to the dance floor.

Her steps lacked their usual precision as half-formed thoughts chased through her mind. Men didn't just haul off and kiss unsuspecting women in her universe. At least, it had never happened to her before. No one had ever dared—not even Jonathan. Especially not Jonathan. Tish had assumed there was something about her, something daunting, that kept men's spontaneous sexual gestures at bay.

She knew that most people regarded her as beautiful, although she didn't take their opinions seriously. In fact, men seemed afraid to try their luck with her even as they clustered around, admiring her from a safe distance. Like Tommy, who was holding her a discreet three inches from his body.

Maybe the expectation that no one would come close without an invitation had given her a touch-me-not air that served to reinforce that pattern...until Mitch. She tripped, missing a step. Mitch had dared.

"You planning a long visit, Tish? Maybe we could see each other."

The dizziness she felt in the wake of Mitch's kiss—not the wine, surely not the wine—made the words sound fuzzy and rather far away. With an effort, she smiled straight ahead, over Tommy's shoulder. Her heels made her just his height, perhaps a shade taller. Aiming for polite ambiguity, she enunciated with care, "My boss gave me a couple of weeks. It was nice of him because I haven't worked there all that long." Losing half a month's salary was going to play havoc with her budget.

"A couple of weeks. Well, would there be room on your agenda for dinner some night?"

Thinking of her budget reminded her of her cheap watch, which reminded her of her earring, which reminded her of Mitch. They'd stood in the middle of the dance floor, in front of God and Aunt Aurelia and everybody and he'd kissed her. Held her in that insultingly loose embrace and *kissed* her.

Tommy's cologne—one of the expensively packaged and heavily advertised varieties, she noted automatically—tickled her nose as he led her through an old-fashioned two-step. He must have taken dancing lessons. Pulled into an expert turn, she spied Pa. His thick gray hair formed a wiry bowl around a bald spot as neat as a monk's tonsure. He was nodding in emphatic agreement as he spoke to an uncomfortably familiar figure. Mitch.

Impossible not to make comparisons, she reflected as she studied the men. Pa was stout and florid, while Mitch—his lean angularity had probably been much the same in adolescence. No doubt he would continue to attract droves of females right out of their wheelchairs if the time ever came for him to retire to a rest home. Mitch looked up and his gaze clashed with hers.

A quiver ran through her. Tommy couldn't help but feel it, she realized, as the boyish contours of his face hardened with self-satisfaction. "Why don't we make it dinner tonight?" he asked. His hand at the small of her back moved microscopically lower.

She stiffened. Somehow Tommy's touch irritated her almost to screaming pitch. He began to draw suggestive circles below her waistband. *There must be something in the Sonoma County air*, she thought in despair. If she had done anything to prompt all this unwelcome sexual aggravation, she didn't know what it was.

He took her silence for assent. "Tonight, then," he said with a satisfied set to his mouth.

Firmly she removed his hands. "Look, Tommy, thanks for the thought, but—"

"But the lady is on her way home with me. Now."

Once again, the easygoing tone of Mitch's voice belied his outrageous words. Tish stared at him in disbelief, anger clearing her head. "You make it sound like—like—"

He leaned close. "What do you want me to say? That you have to sleep it off? Couldn't you maneuver fast enough to get away from this wolf?" he asked in her ear. While she tried to find a shattering retort, Mitch waved casually. "See you, Tommy. Letizia will get back to you."

"Yes, Tommy, call her at my house," Pa said, stepping out from behind Mitch and dismissing Sonoma County's most eligible bachelor with a kindly nod.

"*Mia bambina*, Mitch tells me you're tired from your long drive."

"Mitch's interest in my welfare isn't necessary," she replied tightly. "Honestly, I'm fine. He shouldn't have bothered you."

"You are never a bother to Magda or me, you know that." Pa peered up at her. "There are shadows around your eyes."

Tish ran a finger under one eye. "Mascara. I got a little carried away with all the sentiment at the chapel. I'll just go visit the ladies' room for a minute and—"

"Sorry," Mitch interrupted. "No time."

"Mitch is right. If he's to take you home before he goes to work, you must be on your way," Pa confirmed.

"But I don't need a ride to your house, Pa. I have a car. I can drive myself." Under her breath she added, "In perfect safety and sobriety."

"What did you say?" Pa didn't wait for an answer. "No, no, it's all settled. You must rest. We cannot have you getting sick when we've just got you back, my treasure. Mitch will take good care of you."

Something about Pa's phrasing made her uneasy. "I don't want anybody taking care of me! Including Mitch!" she blurted.

Mitch maintained an impassive expression. "You heard Mr. D'Angeli. Come along, Letizia."

"Don't call me that!"

He looped strong fingers around her wrist and towed her past friends and relatives. "Why not? Don't you like it? It's a pretty name. Unusual."

"I hate it." Did she? Or had she pretended she did in order to fit into an insulated, upper-crust world of Biffs and Buffys for so long that she'd forgotten she was pretending? Right now, Tish wasn't sure.

Guests' eyes widened and mouths gaped as the two of them bolted for the door. "Do we have to rush like this?" she gasped, stumbling in her heels.

"Yeah." He slowed his pace, though. "I've already missed roll call. You can't imagine the razzing I'll take."

"A great big man like you will probably survive . . ." she began, and then caught a fleeting glimpse of Belle's approving grin.

Her cousin called, "Fast work, Sheriff!"

"Sheriff?"

"Sure. Didn't you know?"

"As a matter of fact, I didn't. You're the *sheriff?*"

"Of the whole county," he assured her. His large hands closed around her shoulders to guide her gently through the exit doors.

After the air-conditioning in the hall, the sun's heat struck Tish like a blow. She brushed heavy waves of black hair away from her forehead. The temperature didn't seem to affect Mitch's composure but he asked, "Feeling the heat?" His eyes narrowed. "Can I trust you to wait in the shade while I get my car?"

It would be more embarrassing to go back inside than to put up with his company. "All right, yes," she replied ungraciously.

She watched as he strode away. His movements were economical, fluid . . . predatory. He had a pared-down grace that was unapologetically male. His kiss had been like that, too. Hard. Direct. Not fancy. *Just cataclysmic.*

Mitch pulled up beside Tish and leaned across the seat to open the passenger door. She started to get in, stopped and stared. Metal cylinders littered the seats. "What's all this stuff?"

"These? Speed loaders. Wait a sec, I'll get them out of your way."

Mitch swept the gadgets to the floor, then reached for her hand and tugged her onto the seat.

Tish fumbled with the unfamiliar safety belt and snapped it into place. As the sedan sped out of the parking lot she leaned down and retrieved one of the shiny silver tubes. It was about an inch long and in cross section was daisy-shaped. Holes were drilled right through it in a circle around the center. "A speed loader for what?"

"Bullets," he explained. "You put ammunition in each hole, see, and pop the loaded cylinder in your revolver. Saves time when you need it."

"Oh." She dropped it quickly.

"Don't like guns?"

"Not much. My ex—someone I used to know," she corrected herself, "used to collect them. I've always stayed as far away from them as possible. It bugs me when someone uses a *thing* to establish power over another human being. Money or guns or . . . oh, I don't know."

"Better watch your legs, then," he advised her. "I've got a rifle stowed up against the seat."

Hurriedly she shifted her legs away from the green canvas case. Mitch's frankly approving glance followed the length of thigh revealed when her skirt bunched up, and she straightened the fabric over her knees with a jerk. Her skin tingled as if he'd actually touched it.

Cheerfully he said, "Guns are just tools, Tish. If you know what you're doing and take the right precautions, they won't hurt you."

"Only as dangerous as the people holding them?" She paused. "That's my point."

His laughter filled the car. "It's a problem. A lot of folks are just plain fools. If you're scared of guns—or impressed by them—it's wise to leave them alone." He glanced at her thoughtfully. "Guns and women. They're both explosive. It's all in how you handle them."

She made a rude noise and he smiled.

"No comment? I'm surprised. You don't strike me as the docile type."

That did it. Tish hated being patronized.

"This may come as news to you, but any number of women object to that kind of talk. Including me. You buffaloed Pa into backing you while you kidnapped me, so I'm here. Don't let your ego get all pumped up. I'm sure as hell not intending to be docile, of all things, so— so—" His broad grin brought her to a stammering halt. "So don't even think about it."

"About what?"

The corner of his mouth twitched and she remembered the feel of it on hers, the harsh demands it had made. "About—anything." Tish was annoyed at the distinct break in her reply.

"I said I was surprised." The edge that normally roughened his voice had receded. He'd spoken softly. Tish wondered if he was thinking about the kiss, too.

"Right." She tried to distract herself from dwelling on how dynamite a kisser he was. "Sheriff."

"Does my being sheriff bother you for some reason?"

It did, she realized. His title underscored the disturbing self-confidence of the man. *You can't tell him that*, she thought. It would make her sound fanciful and vulnerable—two things she worked hard not to be. "It makes me feel like an idiot," she said instead. "Why did you let me think you were a deputy?"

He shrugged. "Kind of complicated to explain. I go into uniform two, three times a year. Keeps me close to the other officers."

"Not bad publicity, either," she suggested coolly.

"Not bad at all," he agreed. "Sheriff's an elective office. I can tell my job rubs you the wrong way. Sure you don't have an outstanding warrant against you or something?"

"Positive."

"I could run a check on you," he teased.

She was silent. "I don't think that's funny," she said finally.

"Sorry. Bad joke."

"Yes."

As Mitch turned left to take them through the Valley of the Moon, the handcuffs hooked over the turn-signal lever swung in a wide arc. A quick glance at Tish confirmed that her exotic almond-shaped eyes were following the motion with a kind of incredulous fascination.

He wanted to get a reaction again. "Cuffs turn some women on," he remarked casually.

"How nice for you," Tish said with meticulous courtesy. He was sure that she wouldn't waste so much delicate disgust on someone who bored her. It raised his spirits another notch. "Where do you find women like that?" she went on. "In singles bars? Hanging around the better federal penitentiaries?"

Whatever her capacity for alcohol—a subject he didn't consider closed—Ms. D'Angeli apparently had a low tolerance for innuendo. The indignant flash in her eyes made his ploy worth the price of smoothing things over now. "I don't see the inside of meat markets too much. Frankly I don't like watching people drink. My bailiwick is more the county courthouse. I do get down to the lockup every once in a while, but I don't recall meeting any great-looking women there. Not like you."

He gave her a brief, steady glance. Tish rejected dozens of possible answers for an equally brief, "Thank you."

Was he a teetotaler? Sitting down to dinner without a pleasant glass of something seemed almost abnormal to her. "You disapprove of drinking?" she asked finally.

"I've seen the results when it gets out of hand."

"Traffic accidents and things," she suggested, striving to be fair. Not everyone was raised in a household of grape growers, she reminded herself, and then bit her lip. She'd remembered what Belle had said about his wife.

"And things," he agreed evenly.

He didn't elaborate. It violated all of Tish's canons of conduct to mention his lost family when Mitch had failed to do so, and instead she looked down at her hands. The black numerals on her digital watch swam slightly out of focus. "When is your roll call?"

"Two."

She lifted her wrist closer to her face to make sure she was reading the numerals correctly. "Uh, Sheriff, I hate to be the one to break this to you, but it's closer to four o'clock."

"Yeah, I know."

"Then why all the malarkey about getting to work on time?"

"Even though I'm not going to make it to the shift change, I still have to report in sometime."

"But you made it sound like life and death! What was the big idea, dragging me off from Nonna and Pa's party?"

"Letizia—all right, don't get all riled up, I won't call you that—Tish, I've seen you behind the wheel."

She folded her arms and glared. Mitch looked away from the road for a moment. His gaze fell to where her light summer jacket opened with carefully tailored casualness to showcase the designer blouse beneath. Her arms tightened in an automatically defensive gesture. Instead of hiding her ample breasts the motion pressed them upward.

A sharp breath whistled between his teeth.

"Lady." Mitch sounded winded. "Don't do that while I'm driving."

Tish looked down. Her bosom was straining against her blouse. As required by modesty and an inspection by Nonna, the fabric was opaque. It was also so expensively sleek that it outlined every whorl of the lacy bra she wore underneath it. With a gasp, she dropped her arms to her sides.

"It's nice to be right," Mitch said, facing forward.

"What do you mean?"

"I was pretty sure you weren't one of the boys."

More than anything, Tish wanted to put a little distance between herself and this domineering man. Frosty dignity would do it, she thought. But despite her resolve, she laughed. "Thanks a lot. Are you always crude?"

"That's me. Does it bug you? I can try to watch it." His smile seemed to promise Tish all sorts of things she shouldn't be thinking of after one afternoon's acquaintance.

"Don't you think it's a bit soon to be talking about changing behavior patterns?" she murmured. Inwardly, she cringed. Nothing she said today was coming out the way she intended. Rather than irony, the soft question had a tentative tone, a quality as suggestive as an invitation.

"Yeah, I do," Mitch agreed, startled. "Look, locker-room humor's a habit you fall into in the department. We're kind of a closed society, and the joking can get rough. People who live on the edge need ways to release some of the tension."

"And you like it, that kind of edge?"

They drove through a tunnel of eucalyptus trees and up the D'Angeli driveway.

Tish wasn't sure what was putting the butterflies in her stomach—the acrid-sweet scent of the leaves or her uncertain emotions.

It's a good enough substitute for real life, Mitch almost said aloud. The thought had come out of nowhere. Of course his job was real life. It was the only life he had, or wanted.

When Mitch didn't answer, Tish continued, "Doesn't working under tension all the time get to you?" There, she'd done it again, said something far too personal.

He parked in the curved drive in front of the old-fashioned porch. "That's why we need a release sometimes," he repeated blandly. Unsnapping his seat belt, he turned to face her. His long legs shifted in the confined space, their muscles standing out under the tan cloth. Quickly she looked away and her glance rose to his lap where his pants were neatly zipped. A wave of the melting lassitude she'd felt on the dance floor rushed and ebbed through her, leaving her with the feeling that her bones were the consistency of warm taffy. She looked up at his face. A tiny scar bisected his chin; she tried to concentrate on that.

Reasonably Mitch pointed out, "I'm perfectly willing to cop a plea to being crude. But when I made my remark, you, Ms. D'Angeli, giggled."

"I—I—" She shifted to the attack. "Furthermore I despise guns. Human beings should meet each other as equals, not separated by power games."

"You really like to talk in circles, don't you." It was a statement rather than a question. "Look, I don't want to play any games with you. At least, not those kinds of games."

If only he would leer or do something predictable or unpleasant, she thought. Then she could write him off as a boor and get over this inappropriate physical response. Instead he sat there, not even trying to touch her, devastating her with his honest sexuality. He didn't even pretend to want more than a playmate; didn't attempt to offer the insincere assurances of grand passion that lesser men used in their seductions. He had no need to. A doubt nibbled at her. *No girlfriend?* It hardly seemed possible.

He probably knew more games than she'd ever heard of. Certainly his expertise at bending others to his will couldn't be questioned. Look how easily he had kidnapped her. . . .

"In broad daylight, in front of my entire family." She smiled reluctantly.

"Actually, no, that's not what I had in mind," he replied, puzzled.

She didn't bother to explain. "It might simplify matters if you'd come out and say what you do have in mind."

"We could start with dinner. There are some nice restaurants in Petaluma. We could see how things go from there."

Tish looked out the window, stalling. The two-story house she'd grown up in had become shabby over the years. There was nothing she could put her finger on, no specific sign of neglect, and yet the cheerful yellow paint showed minute cracks, leaving the plain building looking worn. Scarlet rambler roses climbed the west side in eye-pleasing profusion, but bare spots interrupted what had once been a solid curtain of color. Although impeccably mown and edged, the patch of lawn could have benefited from a good watering. Pa's grass used to be vivid green.

She turned back to face Mitch. "I get the feeling you have a definite goal in mind."

His lip jutted out. "Yeah." He touched the ends of her hair then—a light caress at her shoulder. "I can't see much point in beating about the bush. I'm thirty-eight years old. We've both been grown-ups a long time. Of course, I want to find out if anything physical is going to happen between us. Any guy would."

Slowly she shook her head. She wasn't sure which part of his statement she was denying.

"Trust me on this one," he suggested easily. A fingertip wandered lazily through her hair until it found and traced the shell of her ear. A warm shiver rippled down the side of her neck. The delicate investigation stopped at her lobe. Very gently, his thumb joined the finger to rub the tiny hole meant for a pierced earring.

The car was suddenly too small, too hot. Tish pulled frantically at the door handle.

"Tish? What is it? Are you sick? All that wine—"

His quick concern fueled her panicky determination to get out. He leaned across her to give the handle the appropriate twist and in seconds she was standing on the crushed-shell driveway, clutching her purse and breathing deeply.

As swiftly as it had arisen, the panic subsided. Tish faced Mitch, who emerged more slowly and approached her with the same wary care he'd shown when she'd been another potentially dangerous traffic stop.

"Look, Mitch, maybe we'd better not p-pursue this."
She babbled on. "I'm not going to be around that long
and, really, you don't want to waste your money taking me to a restaurant because, well, if we're going to
be crude, I should warn you I don't put out on the first
date."

"I could probably wait for the second. Or even
longer," Mitch informed her softly. Her poise had to-
tally collapsed. Her mouth trembled with a vulnera-
bility that stopped him in his tracks. She was going to
hate him for witnessing how fragile her defenses really
were. He knew *he* would if their circumstances were
reversed, and a conviction had already taken root in
him that they were a lot alike. They both had built walls
that kept each of them safe—and alone.

But if ever a woman needed to be kissed and cuddled
and told how beautiful she was, and then urged to
flower beneath a man's hands . . .

He sighed. "I'd like to get in touch with you in case
you change your mind. Ah, hell, I sound like good old
Tommy, don't I?"

She managed a shaky smile. "No. Not at all.
But . . . there's something wrong."

"What's that?"

"I can't get in. No key."

"No problem." Mitch found a funny wire tool in his
car and inserted it gently into the lock of her grandparents' front door. It clicked open. "See? Your friendly
Sheriff's Department is ready to oblige."

She'd just bet it was. Suddenly, Tish was exhausted.
Murmuring something, she didn't know what, she

fought not to weave on her feet. "I guess I am tired, after all."

"I can see that," he said. "I'll call you."

"Mitch . . . okay."

As she stumbled up the stairs to her old bedroom, Tish thought, *You can call. I don't have to answer.*

5

HE DIDN'T CALL.

Tish was astonished that she slept until the next morning, waking to high coastal fog and sporadic bursts of loud bird song. She lay in the chaste twin bed covered up with the Madras throw she'd picked out when she was a teenager and contemplated the odd occurrences of the day before.

Maybe the wine had hit her, after all. Although she almost never felt its effects to any great degree, she didn't claim to be superhuman. No one could drink indefinitely and not end up drunk, but she hadn't been overindulging by her standards and yet she'd shed inhibitions that had taken a lifetime to form.

Strangely enough, she'd relaxed her rigidly maintained formality to tease and criticize Mitch as she would a brother. Well, no, she corrected, not like a brother. That was the heart of the puzzle. She'd never guessed that some part of her was waiting to melt into a soft, sensual puddle because a man danced with her. Nor had she imagined that a kiss—not even a long or passionate kiss—could disrupt her equilibrium to the point where she couldn't see straight.

It wasn't that she didn't like lovemaking. She liked it just fine; at least, she had before Jonathan turned from her to his flock of secretaries. Given the possibly lethal consequences of promiscuity in an age of untamed viruses, it was just as well he'd lost all interest in her soon after their marriage. Couldn't fit me into his schedule, she thought, amazed at her own lighthearted indifference.

The few carefully selected dates she'd accepted since the divorce had been pleasant. Nothing more. Nice guys, but none of them had knocked her socks off or made the earth move even the tiniest bit. Not like Mitch. She groaned out loud at the sheer craziness of her response to the sheriff of Sonoma County.

Tish punched her pillow and flopped into it facedown. The feeling of being enveloped reminded her of the slow dance they'd shared, of the aching pleasure he'd roused in her. Even if four glasses of wine were responsible for her woozy compliance, in the privacy of her old retreat Tish could admit that it was Mitch's kiss that had ignited the alcohol in her bloodstream. The danger wasn't in the wine; what intoxicated her was Mitch.

And that would never do.

If anything had been necessary to convince her that Mitch Connor ought to be avoided like a particularly disagreeable form of the plague, the interior of his car should have done it. The man needed only seconds to turn himself into a walking arsenal. Those lethal gadgets he surrounded himself with might be no more than the tools of a sheriff's trade, but to Tish they represented the desire to dominate. And she had no intention of allowing herself to fall under a man's thumb. Not now. Not ever again.

She stuck out her tongue at the fluorescent stars Pa had painted on the ceiling twenty years ago and flung back the light Madras cover.

Someone had placed her suitcase just inside the door. Blessing her unknown benefactor, Tish stripped off the slip she'd worn for the short nap she had planned to take yesterday afternoon and pulled on shorts and a top.

She went down the stairs and to the back of the house. Nonna sat at the kitchen table, listening to the radio. The chrome rectangle was as sturdy and ugly as ever. Tish patted it affectionately and reached into the cupboard for a coffee cup.

"Thank you to whoever brought in my suitcase."

"Belle's Frank did that."

"That was nice of him. Is my car outside?"

"It is at the hall as far as I know."

"You're still surrounded by violins, Nonna."

"I like my music." Nonna regarded her benignly. "You used to call it elevator music."

The homogenized arrangement of a popular forties' torch song swirled around them. Tish overfilled her cup and had to take a cautious slurp of the scalding liquid before she trusted herself not to spill. She carried her cup to the table and slid into a seat across from her grandmother. Plastic crackled under her bottom. "Is all my teenage wisdom going to come back to haunt me?" She made a face. "I suppose I deserve it. Go ahead. What other smart-as—I mean, smart-alecky opinions did I dump on you and Pa?"

Ignoring the swearword with a well-directed, silent, pointed reproof, Nonna drank her own coffee. "You were never a wishy-washy sort of girl."

"I was a brat."

Nonna's lips pursed, and Tish watched as a thousand wrinkles deepened. "That spirit was something Gus and I were sad to see disappear from you. It reminded us of your father, when he was a young man. Passion is an important part of life."

Tish looked away. Daddy had been Nonna's only son. She detected a fifteen-year-old sadness in the serenity of her grandmother's voice. Tish tried to speak lightly. "I'm shocked, Nonna. Such a thing to say."

"You don't need to tease. You've never heard me complain about the passionate side of marriage," Nonna said, changing moods instantly. She smiled with deep contentment. Tish's mouth fell open, and she bent over her cup so the loose waves of her hair would hide her smile. So, Nonna and Pa had shared a very private anniversary celebration last night. Good for them.

"However, when I say passion I'm not necessarily talking about the relations between a man and a woman. Other subjects can inspire passion. Art, movies, grapes, famine, war. Music," Nonna continued.

"I guess I outgrew those old judgments. Or had them beaten out of me."

"He *beat* you?" Bright angry patches appeared on Nonna's withered cheeks.

"No, I didn't mean it that way," Tish cried in alarm. Nonna's color slowly returned to normal. "I meant that after a while, life sort of encourages you to be more tolerant of other people's tastes, that's all. Who am I to tell the world, or my much-beloved grandmother, what kind of music to like? And don't think too badly of Jonathan." There were things worth lying for, like keeping Nonna's blood pressure down. Still, out of long habit, she tried to phrase her words so they weren't quite a lie. "He never raised a hand to me."

"He should have given you a fairer settlement."

"I told you over the phone, I got as much as I asked for. It didn't seem right to go after more money when the fault was as much mine as his." She could tell Nonna this with total honesty: "I married him for the wrong reasons."

"All your pretty things gone. Have you sold them?"

Trust Nonna to notice. Tish nodded ruefully. "But you can guess why. I needed something to live on. Now I'm putting everything I can into savings."

"He was an adulterer."

The note of finality in Nonna's pronouncement made Tish shiver. She tried for humor. "On a grand scale. Very top drawer. And, let's face it, I'm bottom drawer."

"You aren't to talk about yourself that way, Letizia! I will not have it!"

Tish laughed with genuine amusement. "I'm not putting myself down. What I mean is, the Kellers' way of life is very sophisticated—"

"Shallow."

"Different, okay? And I was attracted to it. The Old Money, the illusion of security. The trade-off was that I was expected to be a—kind of department-store mannequin, always dressed just so, hanging on my husband's arm so he could score a few social points over the other guys on the polo team. He didn't really want me—just someone who looked like me. He wanted an example of how irresistible he was to women. One of those life-size inflatable dolls with the big chests would have done as well."

"Oh, my baby. My poor darling."

"No," Tish corrected her gently. "I collaborated. I was so sure life in the rarefied atmosphere of Hillsborough would be heaven. So I lunched and wore little hats with veils, and never asked myself who my husband was sleeping with, because it sure wasn't me." She smiled painfully. "I forgot you have to work to get to heaven, not marry into it."

Nonna took Tish's hand in hers. "You did work at it. We saw, Gus and I, when we came to visit, how you tried to please all those Kellers."

"I'm sorry I didn't drive up to see you more often. Jonathan's people thought—well, they thought the family was a bad influence on me. Whenever I came up with an idea they hated, they blamed it on my upbringing and my general lack of aristocratic genes."

"The D'Angelis are peasants. Peasants back to the Ark. And proud of it!"

"Yes, Nonna. That's what they said. Especially when I wanted to get a job. It's a good thing they owned that winery for me to dabble in. At least I could use my degree in wine making in the lab and make a real contribution even if I never got credit for it."

"Ah. That merlot you put out two years ago was extraordinary. Gus and I..." Nonna lifted her cup, tsking at the wet ring left on the table. She rose slowly, waving Tish back when she started to get up. "I shouldn't sit too long. Bad for my circulation. Do you want breakfast?"

"Cereal will do fine." Tish wanted to spare her the extra work.

"I'm making you bacon and eggs," Nonna replied firmly. "Toast made from nice pantone. And hash browns. You've let yourself get thinner than you should. You have no hips at all."

Tish slumped as far as the rigid chair would allow, smiling mistily. "You'll spoil me. It sounds too good to pass up, though. I'm starving. It must be because I skipped dinner. Was the rest of the reception wonderful last night? I'm sorry I missed it."

"It was delightful. But you needed your sleep more than a party." Nonna refilled the coffee maker.

"I guess so. That seemed to be the consensus anyway, and I slept right through. Not more coffee? It's bad for you, Nonna."

"I'm too old to worry about caffeine. Quitting would probably kill me. Leave me my vices, child. They're few enough, God knows."

"Yes'm." The interrogation appeared to be over. Tish had known she wouldn't be able to keep much from her grandmother, but somehow today she didn't mind. It felt good to share some of the hurtful memories, get them out of the way. Still . . . "How many of the family know what I'm saving my money for?"

"Just Gus and me." Nonna sliced a small, yeasty-smelling loaf studded with fruit. "We don't discuss you with the others."

"Thanks," she murmured. "I feel, oh, sort of shy about it. I guess I will till it's a reality, who knows how many years from now. My own winery that nobody can take away." She hesitated. "Has anybody phoned for me?"

Opening the refrigerator, Nonna shook her head, the snowy chignon pinned firmly into place at her nape moving from side to side. "Are you expecting a call?"

"No. That is, sort of. Actually, yes." Intercepting a look from her grandmother that said clearly how gauche she sounded, Tish sighed. "I mean, yes. The sheriff said he'd be calling. For dinner or something, probably."

"A good man. Lonely. Virile." Nonna's voice was sweetly approving.

"Nonna, please."

"Sometimes the obvious needs to be pointed out." The sweetness in Nonna's voice intensified.

Tish straightened, eyes narrowing to suspicious slits. "You're not matchmaking, are you?"

"Good heavens, Letizia. Surely you're capable of getting your own dates."

"Completely," she said with emphasis. "It so happens I'm not interested in a social life right now. While I'm here I'd rather concentrate on being with you and Pa. Where is he this morning?"

"Checking the vines, of course. He wants everything to be perfect when you see them because... Well, you'll understand in a little while. We'll go out in the fields after you eat."

HE DIDN'T CALL.

Mitch glared at the phone on his desk. The county provided him with the latest in electronic toys and this one had enough features to keep an engineer puzzled for a week. One of its simplest functions was automatic dialing; a flick of one finger would ring the D'Angelis' number.

He scratched his forehead instead.

An exciting woman, Tish D'Angeli. No doubt about it. The embodiment of a male fantasy. A precisely detailed mental vision of her long legs and full breasts made him shift in his chair to ease the muscles in his groin. The memory of her firm flesh lifting to create a lacy tattoo on her silk blouse stirred his imagination as nothing had since he'd been an overstimulated teenager. He wanted to unbutton every tiny, fiddly, fabric-covered button, expose her fragrant skin inch by smooth inch, investigate each hidden curve and hollow until he knew them all by heart. His pen slipped out of his hand. Startled, he realized that his fingertips had been stroking small circles on the desk. He grabbed the pen before it rolled over the edge and rubbed his hand against the side of his neck. It was fever-hot. Yes, Ms. D'Angeli was potent stuff. *Whew!*

"I know you're hiding out in here, Mitch, but—"

Suzie pushed the door open and sauntered in.

Mitch grimaced. "You're right. I don't want to be disturbed."

"One of the county supervisors is on line four."

"Let the watch commander handle it."

"The supervisor said—"

"I don't care what he said. I'm on vacation. Like in the song, V-A-C-A—"

"Sure. Your idea of vacation is more work. People on vacation have no business roaring into the office and then slamming doors and refusing to talk to anybody.

They are supposed to use their off time relaxing and getting in a good mood so they don't yell at their hard-working office staff. But instead, *some* people dress up in uniform and cruise around looking for trouble—"

Mitch knew he ought to use his vacation to . . . to . . . The only idea that came into his head was lolling somewhere with a very special brunette. He scowled. So every year he spent his three free weeks going after traffic violators. So what? There were plenty of irre-sponsible drivers who needed to be cleared off the roads. "Can it, Suzie."

"Oh, all right." His secretary fluffed out her frizzy blond hair. "That citizens' recognition banquet is com-ing up. You going to want me to go with you this year?"

He looked at the phone. "It's getting to be a habit, isn't it?"

"Part of the job description. I don't mind. It's sort of a relief going out with a friend who just needs a date. And nobody else takes me anywhere half as nice." She sighed with gusty melodrama. "I only seem to attract poverty-stricken psychology students and guys who work in health-food stores. God, where are all the rich men?" Suzie answered herself: "In this county they're gay. Or confirmed bachelors in love with hedonism. The rest are involved with some strange religion, or they tried marriage once and that was enough for them— Oh, damn, Mitch, I'm sorry. My big mouth."

The phone sat squarely in the center of his desk. One touch, one more fingerprint on the chrome button marked Gus And Magda . . . "It's okay, Suzie. Never mind."

"If you say so." She sounded doubtful. "Let me know about the dinner, would you? I'll need to find something to wear."

That remark penetrated his preoccupation. "If you're doing me the favor, I ought to buy you a dress."

Suzie considered. "I might let you. I've worn the knit thing about a zillion times. The kind of outfit I need for these glitzy receptions, I'll never get a chance to wear except when I go out with you. When are you going to find a real girlfriend?"

"Aren't we getting kind of personal here?"

Her outthrust chin made her look like a pugnacious but cute bulldog. "Trying."

"You applying for the position?" He wasn't worried about the answer. Suzie was a safe bet. Her ambition to marry money had been loudly advertised from the first day she'd been promoted out of the secretarial pool. His own perfectly satisfactory salary didn't approach the dimensions she claimed to find necessary in a potential mate.

"No way. Just being your secretary is hard time." She clapped a scarlet-taloned hand to her mouth. "Oh, no, the supervisor! He's still on line four!" She ran.

Mitch's smile faded as the door swung shut with a pneumatic whoosh. It was easier to take Suzie to the civic functions he had to attend than to go alone and put up with heavy-handed jokes about the absence of an obligatory female at his side. And he'd never been uncaring or unwary enough to invite any of the women he'd dated since Carol's death. At least Suzie knew the emotional score. Escorting a real date to a public function could raise some pretty hairy expectations. When

Mitch asked a woman out, his intentions were limited. Strictly limited. Pleasant company, perhaps mixed with a little mindless sex.

The word sex could be applied to Tish D'Angeli. Her haunting face and lush figure inspired images of long, drawn-out explorations of honey-colored skin and an urgent roller-coaster ride of lovemaking. *Damn. Very, very sexy. Mindless? Definitely not.* After yesterday, he was convinced that there was a nice person inside the sensually appealing wrappings. She was vulnerable under the glamour and the pride; not the sort of woman to accept a quickly-ended affair for the simple, manageable sexual encounter it was supposed to be. She wouldn't be an easy woman to leave. The thought took Mitch by surprise. He suppressed it. Long-term relationships with women weren't for him. They didn't mix well with police work, and he wasn't very good at them anyway.

Friendship with Gus and Magda added a complication. He'd met them at one of the campaign teas that were the bane of an elected official's existence. A stranger to strong family ties, Mitch had been drawn, picnic by picnic, Sunday dinner by Sunday dinner, into the round of celebrations the D'Angelis enjoyed. Gus liked a party. Before long Mitch had become a fixture at their gatherings, even willing to tolerate the constant presence of alcoholic beverages in order to feel the warmth, the sense of belonging.

Come to think of it, he'd seen Tish's picture on the mantelpiece at Gus and Magda's. A high-school photo, probably—a grainy black-and-white that almost concealed her bright, defiant expression. He'd seen that look in her eyes yesterday. By no stretch of the imagination could Mitch consider the granddaughter of the D'Angelis for a casual fling. What Nonna would say if she even suspected he was thinking such a thing made him wince. Her sugar-coated sarcasm would be just the beginning. Mitch didn't want to hurt Nonna and Pa, and treating Tish with what her family would regard as disrespect would be the surest way to do it.

And Tish didn't just drink wine, she *made* the damned stuff. Somehow the image of her smooth complexion got confused with a memory of his mother's face, skin prematurely aged, veins visible around her nose. The face of a long-time alcoholic. People like Tish just didn't know what demons they were letting loose on the world when they made wine.

But, oh God, he liked the way she felt in his arms.

He looked at the phone, but he didn't call.

6

TISH'S HEART LEAPED when Pa handed her the phone. She paused a moment to let her skipping pulse return to normal. It was just the surprise, she told herself firmly. After three days, she'd given up expecting to hear from—

"Oh. Hi, Tommy." She wasn't disappointed, she was . . .

"Hi, yourself. Glad to hear from me?"

Good manners took over. "It's nice of you to call. How are you?"

"Fine. Thinking of you. How would you like to go to a dinner with me? It's a political thing. . . ."

Tish tried not to sigh directly into the receiver. *Oh, why not?* Tommy was certainly presentable. If she went out with him, Nonna might stop making her disconcerting remarks about Mitch's virility. And Tommy wasn't really a jerk—at least he hadn't been in high school. The two of them had had fun together all those years ago, even if sparks hadn't flown. Not at all like when she was with . . .

She tried to sound enthusiastic. "Dinner sounds wonderful."

"Awright! It'll be dressy."

"I can manage."

Tommy laughed as if she'd said something witty. He talked for a few more minutes and then hung up.

Pa was standing right behind Tish where he could hear every word. His raised eyebrows and pursed mouth made him look more than ever like an inquisitive, slightly worldly monk.

Tish dropped a kiss on his bald spot. "Dinner. With Tommy DeCarlo. Tell Nonna, would you, so she'll stop worrying about my social life."

Pa grinned. "DeCarlo, eh? You could do worse, I suppose. If it is a good time you want, come with me to Russo's for lunch. Magda goes to bingo. Come, eat, drink a little vino, enjoy. My treat."

She laughed. Pa's favorite watering hole could not, by any stretch of the imagination, be called a "treat." "You mean that old place hasn't been condemned?" At his hurt look, she improvised quickly, "I mean, I can't wait to see it again. Great! Let's go!"

The roadhouse was still surrounded by garbage cans that smelled strongly of yesterday's food. Inside, it was as much grocery store as saloon, with aisles made crooked by haphazard piles of dried Italian imports spilling off the shelves. The smoke-filled taproom was at the rear. All of Pa's cronies stood to greet her with the instinctive courtesy that made her feel welcomed and valued.

"What can I get for you from the bar, Letizia?" asked Mr. Fontana.

"Please don't bother. I'll drink whatever you're all having." She nodded at the bottle already on the table. He pulled out his handkerchief to rub the streaks off a glass and then filled it with Chianti, which he presented with a flourish. Tish smiled her thanks. "I can remember the first time Pa brought me here. He ordered me a Shirley Temple and every one of the patrons stopped and watched the barman bring it over. I think it must have been the only pink fizzy drink with pieces of fruit in it ever served in this place."

"A historic occasion," Mr. Fontana agreed. Pa nodded, smiling.

The walls were hung with what Tish privately thought of as pieces of dead animals, although she wouldn't dispute her companions' taste by calling the hunting trophies any such thing out loud. The head of a fawn was mounted over the doorway, its expression one of patient resignation. Tish knew just how it felt. "Is the specialty of the house still tripe?" she asked with foreboding.

A stage whisper from Pa drew Tish's attention. "Look who's here!"

She glanced at the man skirting the crowded tables. Furious, she muttered, "Pa, did you set this up?"

"No, truly, Letizia." He sounded puzzled. "Mitch has never come here before, not that I have heard."

"I shouldn't think so. From what he told me, this isn't his kind of place. He doesn't drink, you know."

Pa shrugged. "So maybe he likes tripe."

Cow's stomach? Not likely, Tish thought. She decided to drop the subject of differing tastes. Besides, Mitch had reached their table.

Her breath caught. The sheriff was as tall and lean and imposing as she'd remembered him. Mitch laid his wide-brimmed hat on the cleanest section of the red-and-white checkered cloth. He exchanged greetings with the men and his gaze met and held hers. There it was again—that sharp jolt of awareness, as if her senses were startled completely awake only when he came near enough to activate them.

Why had she thought Russo's so bad? Oddly, the dim light suddenly seemed soft and flattering. The swirling cigar smoke thickening the air took on lazy, appealing patterns. Even the strong ethnic tavern smells of recycled olive oil, pungent tobacco and spilled liquor no longer bothered her.

"Hello, Mitch."

Mitch watched her full lips slowly curve into a smile and felt as if he'd been jabbed in the solar plexus. His breath stopped somewhere in his throat. His brain stopped functioning.

She was beautiful. Her face, her lush body... God, so beautiful. Her smile had dazzled him before, too, but it had just delivered the knockout punch. Her white teeth weren't quite even; an eye tooth on one side slanted a bit, adding a reassuring imperfection to her raven-haired beauty. It was a smile that promised warmth, a safe haven—things he'd done without, it seemed to him, forever.

Tardily he answered, "Hi."

Tish sensed the others exchanging glances and her cheeks warmed. "Are you joining us?"

"Sheriff, take my seat," offered Mr. Fontana, getting up immediately. Tish looked for her grandfather. He was leaning over the bar, talking in the white-aproned barman's ear.

"I just stopped for a minute when I saw Gus's car outside," Mitch began.

Pa heard him, turned and thumped him on the back. "Nonsense. Stay. Have lunch. It's all ordered. Sit here next to Letizia."

Tish watched Mitch's cheeks darken a shade—perhaps due to irritation at their boozy surroundings or his awareness of the older men's curiosity.

"I can't stay," he said, still looking at her. Nervously she ran her tongue several times over her dry lips. Mitch's chest rose and fell as if he'd just sprinted a mile, and without further protest, he slid into the empty seat beside her.

"I am glad to see you, Mitch." Pa's hoarse voice sounded more strangled than usual. "Joe Fontana has a car he's working on. He wants us to look it over with him. It would bore Letizia. You can keep her company for lunch. I will be back to pick her up in an hour and a half or so...."

With Mitch's gaze on her, Tish scarcely noticed her grandfather and his friends filing out until she realized that she and Mitch were alone at the table. "They're gone," she observed unnecessarily.

"Yeah." Mitch stirred, his rapt look fading. He scanned the interior of Russo's with unconcealed distaste.

"You don't have to stay here if you don't like it." She spoke quietly, so the criticism wouldn't carry to the other noontime patrons. "I think this place is the downside of funky, myself."

He unclenched his jaw enough to talk. "No problem." The tightness in his tone made her wince. She twisted the thick stem of her wineglass between restless fingers.

"I take it this isn't one of your usual hangouts, is it, Sheriff?"

Her question dragged a hint of a smile from him. "Can't say that it is. What a dump. It smells like a distillery."

"Shh. That's Mr. Russo behind the bar. It's not so bad."

"Your kind of place?" His demand was incredulous but low-voiced.

"It's not Chez Panisse, I'll admit. The dead animals add a certain something to the ambience that I could do without. Otherwise it's all right since—" Ingrained wariness and profound female instinct stopped her. She couldn't say, *since you came in*. She substituted, "I don't mind it too much. As long as nobody expects me to eat tripe."

"You're in luck then." Mr. Russo grinned as he walked up to the table, carrying a tray piled with platters. "Antipasto, salad, minestrone, ravioli—"

Mitch sat in silence as Mr. Russo arranged the plates and bowls in front of them. "And for the sheriff to drink?" he asked.

"Milk," Mitch growled.

"Certainly."

Tish didn't try to make further conversation. She kept her gaze fixed firmly on her lunch as she ate. She looked up only when she reached for the antipasto platter or soup tureen to make sure her hand wouldn't brush Mitch's if both of them wanted a slice of salami or a ladleful of minestrone at the same moment. She was afraid of what might happen if their hands touched. The tamped-down anger obvious in Mitch's every overcontrolled movement wasn't something with which she wanted even fleeting, accidental contact. Yet she wanted to touch him, massage the tension out of his body, stroke the sun-kissed skin—

"Can't you eat?"

"What?" Tish looked at her raised fork, which was poised motionless halfway to her mouth with a piece of ravioli on it. She put it down. The metal clattered against her plate. "It's—a bit salty."

Mitch pushed his chair back with a scrape of wooden legs on linoleum. "Let's get out of here, then. We can roost among the garbage cans while we wait for Gus."

"You don't have to wait at all—"

"I changed my mind. I want to wait, all right?" The aggressiveness of his admission might not be directed at her but it stung just the same. His tone gentled. "I stopped by to see Gus on an impulse. Maybe I drove by this dive because I knew he spends time here, I don't know. Maybe I thought he'd mention you. You've been on my mind."

"You didn't call," she barely whispered.

His lips framed the word *no*. Tish couldn't look away. "The result of too much thinking. I came up with some good reasons why we shouldn't see each other. We can talk about them outside."

A wave of disappointment unsettled the heavy food in her stomach. Tish sat rigidly in her chair for a few seconds as she fought a wave of nausea. He didn't want to investigate the impact they seemed to have on each other. Tish was fairly sure the ravioli would stay where it belonged. Ridiculous to become so upset because his conclusion matched her own. Life would be much,

much simpler without a sexy sheriff complicating it, and apparently he felt the same about her intrusion into his existence. She bent to retrieve her purse.

Mr. Russo bustled over with irregular-shaped balls of lemon sherbet nested in stainless-steel bowls. "Now, where are you going so soon? Have your dessert, on the house for a beautiful lady who doesn't honor us with a visit often enough."

Tish glanced up at Mitch helplessly. Rejecting his offer would be rude. From where she sat, Mitch looked tall and authoritative. She bit back a sigh. Mitch didn't need the psychological advantage of extra inches. He was impressive all by himself. He was also irritated. She could tell from the way he carried himself, all coiled up. Ready to lash out?

"Thank you," Mitch said, too evenly but with creditable politeness. Over the years of her marriage, Tish had learned to tense at the threat of public displays of anger. She relaxed a trifle at Mitch's calm tone. "Tish?"

"Yes, thanks, Mr. Russo. How thoughtful of you." She smiled warmly with relief and settled back into her chair to find Mitch watching her.

"If you smiled at me like that, I'd bring you a truckful of lemon ice cream."

"Sorry. I can't be bought. Not anymore." Before he could question her comment, she plunged on. "I'm glad you didn't refuse to stay. Mr. Russo would have been crushed."

Mitch picked up his spoon. "Yeah, I figured."

It was silly to feel so proud of him all of a sudden, just because he'd done something kind, but Tish did. "What reasons?" she asked softly.

"Hmm?"

"What are the good reasons we should avoid each other? I want to compare them with mine," she explained defiantly. *Don't feel anything for him,* she warned herself. *Too late,* she admitted reluctantly.

Ornery, Mitch thought, and decided to be blunt. "For one thing, I don't much like what you do for a living. And I didn't get the impression you're crazy about my job, either. For another, your grandparents wouldn't be thrilled if they found us in bed together. And, lady, that's where I want to take you."

Tish tasted her sherbet. It pooled on her tongue and then coated her throat with a sugary tang. She tried to tell herself that it was only the icy sweetness making her short of breath. "You're right. I don't like guns, and if my making wine bothers you, well, there's nothing I can do about that." Not that she actually made wine where she worked now. Testing the absorbent qualities of cork was more like it. Someday she'd create her own wines again. At the moment, ambition didn't seem as important as this hushed, intimate conversation with the man next to her. "However, just for the sake of argument, *if* we were going to be—close—I'd do my absolute best to make sure it was as far away from my grandparents as we could possibly get. Tierra del Fuego, say."

"A real lovers' hot spot," he agreed, deadpan. "That's near the South Pole, isn't it?"

"The tip of South America. That might be far enough," she continued. "However, the distance would be for my own peace of mind, not out of necessity. It so happens that Nonna thinks of you as . . . the word she uses is virile. Frankly, I think she and Pa consider you a likely addition to the family gene pool."

He swore fluently.

Unreasonably hurt, she prodded him further. She wasn't canvasing the county for someone to take a dip into the gene pool with, either; but he didn't have to make it so clear that she failed to inspire him with visions of blissful matrimony and a full nursery. "Don't worry, I'm not asking you to marry me. But there's another flaw in what you said. I'm not some bimbo ready to hop into bed just because you snap out an order. I don't like being pushed around."

"I never thought you did," Mitch said, dumbfounded. He leaned over without thinking and used a fingertip to catch a tiny smear of yellow sherbet at the side of her mouth. He was fascinated by the smoothness of her skin, the moistness of her bottom lip. His finger lingered there for a second. "Is that the impression I gave you?"

Her eyes evaded his. "Perhaps not intentionally, but yes."

"This may come as a surprise to you, but I've never hauled out my revolver and ordered a woman to show me a good time in my life. As a matter of fact, behavior like that constitutes rape in this state and just about anywhere else I can think of."

"I know. I didn't mean it that way."

"So what did you mean?" he asked grimly.

When she glanced at him, Mitch's perfectly justifiable sense of offense faded away. Her exotic eyes were clouded, pleading, and he couldn't guess their message. He only knew she couldn't have any idea how open and defenseless she appeared. The strangest impulse shot through him, to tell her it didn't matter, that she didn't have to let down her guard or give him any answers. Hell, he wasn't her keeper or her conscience. He ignored the thought. After all, she'd practically accused him of a felony, one that was exclusively the activity of sleazeballs as far as he was concerned. He deserved an explanation.

Tish spoke slowly. "I didn't mean that I believe you resort to rape to get women into bed." Hardly, she thought. Women probably tried to ravish *him*. "It's only that you're . . . so masculine. . . ."

"Tish, you say it like it's an insult. I'm not prepared to give up being male. I was born this way."

"I can tell." She played with the stem of her wineglass again. "You do have a tendency to make suggestions as if they were orders, that's all."

"You're always free to disagree with anything I say. Usually you do. Would you stop fiddling with that?" She stared at him in incomprehension. Breathing hard, he reached over and lifted the glass out of her hand, shoving it to the far side of the table. The Chianti slopped over the brim, and with a curt exclamation, he whipped a handkerchief from his pocket and scrubbed the liquid from his wrist and cuff.

Mitch got up, reached into his pocket for his wallet and tossed paper money helter-skelter among the dishes. Pressure built up inside him. Tish's eyes were wide, her expression one of amazement, as if she thought him a freak, an outsider, somebody who could never, ever fit in with loving, decent people—the kind she'd grown up with. The pressure blew. "I can't stay in here. I'm suffocating. Tish, my mother is an alcoholic. Ever since I was ten years old, I'd have to search through places like this to find her and bring her home before she had time to drink up the rent money—or find some man to sell herself to in exchange for a bourbon...."

His voice cracked, something that hadn't happened to him in twenty years. He turned on his heel and strode out.

Instinctively Tish started after him, halting reluctantly as Mr. Russo called out, "Letizia, your purse! And this is too much to pay. Anyway, Gus said to put it on his tab!"

"Thanks for the purse. And don't worry about the money. The sheriff must mean for you to have it." She ran down the aisle, dodging boxes of *orzo* and plastic-wrapped containers of dried tomatoes.

In the unrelenting sunshine, she found Mitch unlocking his car—a regulation sheriff's vehicle this time—using quick, angry movements punctuated with colorful obscenities. As he jerked the door open, she said, "You know more cusswords than anyone I've ever met in my entire life."

"Yeah, well, we're agreed, aren't we? I'm a crude kind of a guy. And a bully, and what else? Oh, yeah. A rapist, probably."

His mouth was set in a tight, hard line. *An unhappy line*, she thought. How old had he been when he'd learned to hold his mother's secret in? Ten, or even younger. He must have held on to the flashes of unpredictable humor and buoyant confidence through who-knew-what trials of the spirit. And the sensitivity he spent so much effort hiding had gone underground in sheer self-defense.

She answered the point that seemed to bother him the most. "I never believed you'd—overpersuade a woman." Reaching out, she laid her hand on his arm, feeling the golden hair under her palm. *Soft*, she thought. *Very soft but very male.* His skin was fine-grained, the underlying muscle and bone hard. A luscious, languid heat spread from where her hand touched his arm, through her body.

The warmth reached her knees, and without thinking, she leaned against the car for support.

"Ow!" Tish jerked her elbow away from the hot metal. The open door gave her an unimpeded view of the front seat, where a clear plastic garment bag and its contents lay in untidy folds. She dropped her hand from his arm. "Do you wear blue sequins often?" she asked coldly.

"Yeah," he said with the lack of expression that irritated her. He picked up the bag and shoved it through the back door and onto the seat. "All the time. It's my color, don't you think?"

"Be careful with that! Sequined dresses are notoriously delicate," Tish warned. Embarrassment rushed through her. Why should she try to save some other woman the annoyance of bent and broken sequins? One of *Mitch's* other women?

Her warning somehow defused Mitch's anger. The gentle massage of her palm and fingers had roused a quick response that had gotten mixed up with bitter resentment at himself for revealing things about his childhood he'd never told anyone before. He had stood very still under her ministrations because if he'd moved at all, he would have snatched her to him for a long, hard kiss and the comfort of her body pressed against his aching loins. An action like that would probably convince her that he was the animal she believed him to be.

When she'd exclaimed over Suzie's dress in genuine distress, it occurred to him again how nice she was. An overused word, nice, but the only one he could think of. Nice. Tender, down-to-earth, not impressed with her own beauty, able to be hurt. Real.

She raised a hand to shade her eyes from the sun's glare. Rolling his shoulders to take his mind off his arousal, he thought he must be a brute to keep her out in the sun so long when it seemed to bother her.

"Come on," he said gently. "The car has air-conditioning. Who knows when Gus will get back? Will you trust me to behave myself while you sit with me?"

She studied him warily. He sighed. "The dress is something I picked up for a friend. Not a girlfriend." No point in being too honest; he didn't have to mess things up by admitting he'd paid for it.

Tish hesitated. Sanity returned. It wasn't any of her business whose dry cleaning he carried around with him. She got in. Cool air rushed out of the vents and bathed her face. "Your friend must be thrilled at the way you treat her gown."

Mitch lounged comfortably, one arm slung over the back of the seat. "No complaints yet."

"I'll bet," Tish muttered absently as she peered over her shoulder. She inspected the sky-blue sparkle behind the security glass that separated the front from the rear of the vehicle. A tiny size, a four or six perhaps, and cut and elasticized to hug whatever curves his friend might have. Tish knew that if she were foolish enough to try on a similar style she'd look like an Amazon in a breastplate.

She turned. "No door handles?"

"In back, no. That's where we keep the bad guys. The public frowns on it when we let criminals open the doors and waltz away. So, no handles." His grin flashed briefly. "Oh, I forgot. You don't believe in bad guys."

"Of course I'm aware that dangerous people are out there. I just don't dwell on it. You can get paranoid that way."

"In my business you can stay alive that way."

She tried to settle back and relax. There were no obvious signs of weapons in the front seat. This vehicle was much tidier than Mitch's personal one. Still, the radio was a constant reminder of the car's official function.

She guessed it was inevitable that Mitch, whose early life must have been chaos, had chosen a career that made him the one in control. . . .

"You know," she said with difficulty, "my parents weren't there for me, either. They died."

He closed his eyes, then opened them again. "I'm sorry. I am, Tish. But it's not the same thing. A drunk kills her—himself one drink at a time. When he chooses to drink, he chooses to die."

"Not so different."

He groaned. "Oh, God, honey. I put my foot in it, didn't I? Your parents—"

"They weren't problem drinkers. I didn't mean to give you that impression. Daddy didn't mean to die— he fell off a roof he was fixing. An accident, plain and simple. Mama wasn't so simple. She had this neurological thing...." Tish's voice trailed off. "She'd been sick off and on for a long time. The doctor said she was responding to the medication and ought to live to be ninety. Daddy's accident coincided with one of her flare-ups and all of a sudden she was in the hospital and then she was gone. She didn't want to live without him. So you see, the result is the same as with your mo—any sort of self-destructive behavior. She chose to die." Tish looked at the unlit neon sign, Russo's, with the tilted martini glass that would flash after dark. "They say kids grow up and leave their parents. Really, it's the parents who let go."

Mitch's hands were clenched on the steering wheel. "And you were alone."

Tish found a smile. "Hardly alone. There was quite a battle royal over who'd get me. My grandparents beat out Aunt Aurelia by a hair. Thank goodness. I rebelled enough against Nonna. God only knows what kind of trouble I'd have gotten into with a totalitarian like Aurelia to inspire me to heights of revolt."

Mitch appreciated her attempt to lighten the atmosphere. His hands unclenched. "Right. I can imagine it. Tish D'Angeli, teenage terror."

"Oh, I managed to avoid the classic stupidities. I didn't get pregnant or try drugs or break Pa's heart by registering with a different political party. The worst thing I did was marry the wrong man. We met at agricultural college. He was auditing some classes in viticulture. His family owns a winery, among other things."

"Ah."

"Looking back, I wonder if . . ." Tish tilted her head as she asked herself an entirely new question. Had she accepted Jonathan because he was precisely the kind of man she could never really love? No fear she'd break her heart over anything he ever did, no possibility she'd lie down and die, the way her mother had when she lost her husband.

Mitch's voice interrupted her thoughts. "Gus is pulling into the lot, Tish."

"Well, goodbye, then." She paused. It didn't seem right to leave without some sort of acknowledgment that the time she'd spent with Mitch had been special. As if it were the most natural thing in the world, she leaned over to kiss his cheek. Just a peck, she told herself. Her lips grazed his skin, roughened by the hint of bristly stubble that tasted and smelled of spicy aftershave, before they reached his lips.

Dimly she realized that her position had become uncomfortable, but she didn't care.

This time, he seduced without demanding; his mouth wasn't hard, but gentle, giving. Then his tongue flicked out, and its erotic dance across the edges of her teeth sent shivers up her spine.

Trembling, she pulled away.

Mitch cupped her chin, and she couldn't help moving her face back and forth to feel the calluses at the base of each finger. "Letizia," he muttered. "Honey, I can't believe I'm saying this, but we shouldn't be doing these things. There's too much potential for getting hurt." He didn't say which one of them might be at risk. He didn't need to, she thought. Whether he was about to admit it or not, tough guy Mitch Connor was as susceptible to her as she was to him.

"I know. A mistake." She pressed a kiss into the center of his palm and pulled back. Another long moment passed as she memorized his face, feature by feature. The familiar expressionlessness couldn't defeat her, now that she was sure of his sensitivity. She watched muscles constrict in the powerful column of his throat as he swallowed. No, she wasn't the only one at risk if they saw more of each other.

Her senses clamored for further exploration and it took physical effort not to touch him again. "Goodbye," she repeated, and grabbed her purse.

Mitch watched her walk swiftly across the parking lot and get into Gus's car. *Better this way,* he told himself. The last thing he needed was a woman who manufactured poison for a living and got so persistently, so sensually, under his skin.

And it was a hell of a thing when he couldn't even convince himself of that.

7

"OF COURSE I'M NOT scared to be alone," Tish said.

Pa peered around Nonna, who was adjusting his tie. "I don't like to leave you by yourself. It was fine of Belle and Frank to get us tickets for the play, but not while you're visiting. There are so many crazies out there, you never know who or what might come sneaking around, trying to break in."

"Now, Gus," said Nonna, giving the knot a final twitch and pat, "Letizia is a big girl."

"It's only for the night," Tish chimed in. "I'll be fine. And you look gorgeous. That's a wonderful tie, if I do say so myself. When did I give it to you—1975?"

"A year later. See the flags and pictures of George Washington? It was for the Bicentennial." Pa puffed out his chest to display the artifact more clearly.

"I remember. Wow, did I have good taste. Red, white and electric blue. And so wide! None of those skinny, itsy little ties for me."

He bristled protectively. "This is a fine tie. I love it." Reaching up, he touched Tish's cheek. "I love you for giving it to me."

She covered his hand with her own and squeezed it. "You two had better get a move on. It's going to take an hour and a half to get to San Francisco, and that's if the traffic's light."

"All the cars will be coming this way, away from the city," Nonna said with comfortable conviction. "We'll have the highway south to ourselves and the people trying to go north across the Golden Gate will hate us."

"Let's hope so." In Tish's experience, it was safer not to make assumptions about Highway 101. "I've never been on that route when all the lanes were open. They're always being expanded or repaired or flooded out or something."

Nonna turned to Gus. "You can smoke your smelly old pipe in the car, as long as you leave it there during dinner and the play."

Tish walked them to the garage. Pa grunted with the exertion of lifting the heavy door. She glanced at Nonna, who stood watchful and still. A slight shake of her head stopped Tish from offering to help. Tish didn't relax until Pa turned to them with a smile of triumph and waved his wife through to the car.

"Oh!" Tish ran to the driver's side and leaned through the window just after Pa slammed the door shut. "Pa, if you wait a sec while I get my purse, I could ride with you as far as the hall where you had the reception and pick up my car. I know you said one of the cousins would bring it around, but it's been almost a week."

"Patience, Letizia," Nonna reproved. "The boys' feelings would be hurt if you insist on dashing over to get the car before they have time to do it for you. Besides, you were the one who said Gus and I should hurry."

"I didn't exactly—"

"If Mr. French calls from the bank, tell him we'll call back on Monday. Supper's in the refrigerator. There's

a nice Doris Day movie on the Sacramento channel tonight. Enjoy yourself."

"Terrific." Tish was torn between exasperation and
laughter. "Big Friday night." She waved as they drove
away.

The afternoon breeze rippling inland from the sea
pushed a loose stem of the climbing rose in dreamy
waves so that it looked like a beckoning jeweled arm.
Tish paused to twist the stubborn green strand into
place. A loose-petaled rose brushed against her, leaving its scent and a lingering sensation of velvet on the
inside of her elbow. She rubbed it idly and remembered Mitch's arm, taut and muscular under her stroking hand. Intense longing flooded her and she stared
blindly at the rose.

She tried to think. This was stupid. It was also the
twentieth century. Women didn't wait around for
Prince Charming to favor them with a phone call.
Didn't the glossy magazines assure up-and-coming
feminists that it was practically a social duty to hunt
princes down on their own? If she was so sure she
wanted Mitch, Tish could go out and get him. She could
try phoning, anyway. It wouldn't be hard to discover
if he had changed his mind.

Of course, Mitch Connor didn't give the impression
of being a man whose mind was easily changed. Tish
shook her head. Forget it. Forget him.

And where the hell was her car? Couldn't a couple
of her devoted cousins find an hour to retrieve the
darned thing?

On impulse, Tish walked swiftly into the house and rang a number she found on the list Nonna kept by the kitchen phone.

"Belle? It's Tish.... They just left.... Staying overnight in the city. Uh-huh, Nonna said something about Pa not driving after dark anymore. Listen, do you know which of the cousins was going to go get my car? ...No, it's not an emergency or anything...."

She stood tapping her toe through Belle's admonitions and questions. Taking advantage of the lull when Belle paused to shout at one of her children, she interjected, "I'll admit it, I don't have to rush to the doctor's, the lawyer's or the grocery store. But if I did, I wouldn't be able to because I don't have my car. It's understandable that nobody wants to drop whatever he's doing and race off to bring it over here for me. But if that's the case, I need to make arrangements so I can get out to the hall myself."

"Tish, you're being ridiculous," said Belle cheerfully. "I know for a fact a few of the guys plan to pick it up and drop it off for you."

"When?"

For once Belle sounded disconcerted. "Well—I—cripes, Tish, how should I know? I mean, you can't burst out and ask somebody doing you a favor when they're going to do it. That's rude."

"Is it?" Tish muttered. "Oh, glory, maybe it is. Nonna seems to think so, too. Since I'm not in desperate straits, forget the whole thing. The situation will take care of itself. Either someone'll remember to pick the car up, or it'll get towed."

Belle laughed. "That'd be interesting, wouldn't it? Then you could see the sheriff."

"Is he in charge of towed cars?"

"Who cares? It would make a great excuse, anyway."

"No good. Too obvious." Tish caught at her thoughts. Belle loved gossip. "Besides, who says I want to see him?"

"Get real. Franklin, Jr., aim that water pistol at me and you're losing your hand at the wrist." Tish didn't think her cousin would carry out the threat but apparently Franklin, Jr., wasn't so sure, because Belle returned to their conversation. "What was I saying? Oh—get real, Tish. Mitch is about the right age. How many men are—who aren't creeps or married? He's fantastic looking—"

"He does have a nice smile," admitted Tish.

"He also has a great bod," Belle said blithely. "How is he at kissing?"

"I *beg* your pardon!"

"Just thought I'd ask. Don't have a heart attack. I couldn't help being curious, that's all. Not everybody gets a first kiss in the middle of the hall dance floor. Must have been exciting."

"Oh, all right. It was exciting." Tish added hastily, "Especially when I realized Aunt Aurelia must have been watching. What did she say?"

"You don't want to hear. So the kiss was okay? For Pete's sake, what else do you want in a man? He must make good money, too—top lawman in a county with a population this size. Unless you measure things like that a lot differently from normal people—"

The small salary the conglomerate paid to very junior wine makers popped into her mind. She gave a tired giggle. "No. I'm pretty sure I don't."

"Okay, then . . ."

Tish endured another lecture on Mitch's merits. He was well-thought-of, kind to children. "Of course," complained Belle in a momentary lapse from Mitch-boosting, "he did give Franklin, Jr., the water pistol. But he doesn't have any kids himself, so he probably didn't realize what a pain it can be, getting your behind spritzed when you least expect it." She recovered. "I don't see how you're going to do any better than Mitch Connor."

"Me, neither." An unfamiliar self-doubt made her stomach tremble. A basic weakness, a wish to be connected. Not just to anybody—a certain somebody. To Mitch. Her instant attraction to such a natural-born leader scared her. She'd sworn never to allow herself to be intimidated again. She shrugged restlessly. "None of this makes any difference, Belle. He doesn't want to see me again."

"You've got to be kidding. What's the matter with him?"

The astonished indignation in Belle's exclamation restored Tish's sense of humor. "Gee, Belle, I don't know. I must be resistible."

"Bull—I mean, baloney," she retorted. Franklin, Jr., and his siblings were probably playing near their mother. "You're gorgeous and he noticed it. You wait. He'll show up."

"I'm glad one of us has all this faith in me. Nonna said you and Frank are putting on a barbecue before I leave. . . ."

The change of subject worked. Belle went into great detail about potato salad. Finally, Tish was able to end the conversation and hang up.

Tish went outside to turn on the sprinkler. After several days of assiduous watering, the grass was much greener. Nonna's meticulous housekeeping left little for her to do inside except dust, with one of the used paper towels she found under the sink. Her grandmother, always a thrifty housewife, seemed to have become a compulsive saver. A little sadly, Tish rinsed the rag of paper and hung it on its rack. Nonna was developing the eccentricities of old age, and she'd do her best to accommodate them.

Five days' worth of solid D'Angeli cuisine left her—for once—disinclined to eat supper. Instead she took a walk to the grape fields.

Large leaves curled above dwarfish brown vines that were nearly fifty years old. Hard green grapes were clustered beneath the foliage. September must seem a long way off for growers whose livelihood depended on the right combination of sunlight and water to ripen their crop. Pinot noir, chardonnay, cabernet—each type of grape had an old and beautiful name, and a fragile nature. Not only could the weather keep growers from showing a profit, but their success could be affected by market prices, competition from foreign countries, the vagaries of the public's taste and business decisions by big vintners like the company Tish worked for.

Tish stood stock still. The possible significance of dry lawn, unreplaced rose bushes—and reused paper towels—abruptly occurred to her. She retraced her path. A quick twist shut off the sprinkler. Drops clung to blades of grass, glistening in the last rays of the setting sun.

Water was expensive. Nonna was expecting a call from a banker. It just might be that Tish wasn't the only D'Angeli who happened to be strapped for cash.

Frowning thoughtfully, she wandered inside. The odd, restless feeling came back. The murder mystery she picked up was dull and the television-news broadcasters more inane than usual. In her apartment she would have left the TV on, but, irritated by it here, she switched the set off. In the sudden quiet, she noticed the country noises filtering in through screened windows. A dog barked and fell silent. Bats keened and clicked as they flew over the fields. Occasionally she heard the distant rumble of a car going past the turnoff to Nonna and Pa's long driveway. She sat in the living room and gazed out the picture window at the stars.

The wooden bird in the cuckoo clock had popped out to coo ten when she looked up at the sound of a car approaching the house. Tires crunched over shell and slowed to a stop.

Hesitantly Tish edged to the window beside the door, peeking carefully through the lace curtains that shielded it. The deep quiet outside began to seem ominous. She was alone in a secluded farmhouse, and someone who didn't want to be seen or heard waited out there. Her nervous fingers fumbled for the porch-light switch.

The porch and yard were empty. The driveway was in darkness.

Tish's heart pounded. She huddled against the thick redwood panels of the door, wondering whether she was being overcautious or not. A strange crackle from the direction of the dark driveway, where the invisible

car and its anonymous driver lurked, forced a decision. She dashed for the phone and punched 911.

"He's still out there?" responded the tinny voice after Tish stumbled through an explanation.

"Whoever it is is still there as far as I can tell."

"All right, miss." The operator spoke with such
soothing calm that Tish wondered how terrified she
sounded. "Stay on the line, we're transferring the information to the Sheriff's Department. Don't hang up,
keep the line open.... Okay, there's a sheriff's car in
your vicinity. In fact—"

Tish heard a giggle. "In fact, we seem to have iden-
tified the intruder on your property."

"What should I do?" Tish was thoroughly confused.

The operator responded in a just-between-us-girls
tone. "If it were me, I'd go out and drag him in, honey."

"What—? You mean—?" Light dawned. "I see," said
Tish evenly. "I'm sorry for troubling you."

"Nightie night, now."

Embarrassment mingled with relief and anticipation. She unhooked the chain lock and swung the front
door inward, ready to blast her "intruder"—when the
sight of Mitch stopped her dead.

His head rested against his forearm, which was
propped against the upper bar of the doorframe.
Patches of perspiration darkened his shirt, and soot and
brown stains marred the rest of his uniform. Something was clotted in his hair. He smelled like ashes.

"My God, Mitch!"

He lifted his head to look at her. Tish gasped. From
his stance she'd expected the blankness of exhaustion
or despair. Instead his eyes glittered, his face was rigid
with intense emotion, with a desire so raw that she went

hot, then cold, then hot again, all in an instant. Like a deer caught in the blinding trap of automobile headlights, she couldn't move, couldn't breathe, couldn't do anything to save herself from a responding jolt of desire.

"Needed to see you," he muttered, as if to himself. "Tried to stay away but . . . couldn't. You understand?"

"Yes." She almost didn't recognize the soft, drugged sound of her own voice. "Yes."

Fuzzily Tish tried to think. "You'd better come on in. What happened?"

"Three-car pileup at Denman Flat. Two of 'em exploded. Pieces of drivers splattered everywhere, all over the road. Dear God, Tish . . ."

He went on in a compulsive monotone. Distressed, Tish shut her ears to the details. If she listened she'd be sick, and she couldn't afford any weakness. She needed to help him.

She placed a tentative hand on the fist dangling at his side. Instead of following her into the house, Mitch pulled her to him like a drowning man clutching a life preserver and sank his face into her hair.

His anguished mumbling continued unabated, so she rested her forehead against the hot, damp skin of his neck. The buckle of his thick belt dug into her midriff. Mitch was grimy and smelled overpoweringly of burned gasoline and blood. Tish clung to him, ignoring the discomfort, silently willing him to relax, to let the horror go. After a while, his monologue slowed and Tish began to stroke his back with long, slow sweeps of her hand. A shudder ran through the knotted muscles under her palm.

Endearments spilled from her with a facility that would ordinarily have scared her. "Let's go inside, love. Oh, hon, let me help, sweetheart...."

Arms wrapped around him, she shuffled Mitch into the living room. Without loosening his grip on her, he raised his head. "Sure you want me in here? I don't smell too pretty."

"I don't mind, and I'm the only one here," Tish said, relief at his near-normal tone making her go limp against his chest.

He looked down at her and his grasp tightened until she could hardly breathe. "You feel so good. I can't work up the energy to make myself let go."

"Don't, then, sweetheart."

Their mouths came together hungrily. The need for Tish that had been growing since the day they met burst through Mitch in violent waves. He felt instantly full and ready and wanting. He groaned as the tip of her tongue slipped beneath his to find the secret flesh at the base.

He gasped, "I'm going out of my mind. We have to slow down, babe. I don't want to lose control with you."

Control, she thought, catching her own breath. *Of course.*

She lifted a trembling finger to wipe away a gleam of moisture under his bottom lip. The sensation of slick pliancy was so satisfying that she kept on running her fingertip across the warm wetness until it dried and Mitch grabbed her fingers for a quick kiss.

"That's hardly the way to help me keep control, Tish."

"Maybe I want you to lose it," she whispered. "Fair's fair. I've lost any control I ever had."

He pressed her hand to his cheek. "Damn it, I don't know what's happening to me. I've never felt like this before, not even with Carol—"

His voice broke off. Long, slow shudders began to course through him again, shaking Tish with their intensity.

"Your wife," she guessed softly.

"My wife," he confirmed. "She was pregnant—we'd given up hoping—we wanted that kid more than—more than anything. We lived in L.A. Drunk driver crossed the freeway divider at one o'clock in the afternoon, smashed into her while she was coming home from the doctor's. I was heading home for lunch and I saw this accident—'just another accident'—and stopped to give assistance. She was all covered up by that time but I saw a bracelet on the pavement and picked it up. It was the one I'd given her when we found out we had a baby on the way. The paramedics were there and they were stuffing my life—my whole life—into a body bag while the drunk just stood there, not a scratch on the bastard, the lousy bastard. . . ."

Tish stroked his cheek, pressing herself against him, offering the only comfort she could, because there wasn't anything to say.

After a while, Mitch relaxed his punishing grip. "Thanks. I needed . . ." His brown gaze was bright and blank and bleak. His forced composure brought burning tears to her eyes.

Tish found her voice. "Well, I need you. And like it or not, I think you need me. Please don't close me out. Don't—don't reject me, Mitch."

8

MITCH TOUCHED HER gently—hair, cheekbones, neck, tense shoulders. "Honey, that's the last thing in the world you have to worry about. I want you." A devastating wave of desire flowed through him. His thighs tautened and trembled, while his thickened flesh thrust painfully against his trousers.

Tish gave him one of her slow, beautiful smiles. "I'm glad," she said simply. "Come to bed."

"I don't want to cheat you," he muttered. "I want to make it good for you but, Tish, I'm so close to exploding and I smell to high heaven. . . ."

She kissed the scar on his chin. "I guess you can have a shower. Would that help?"

"One of my problems, anyway."

The reemergence of his sense of humor eased the shared tension and grief. *A warning sign,* Tish thought. When had she begun to care so much? Pushing the question away, she found towels for him.

Mitch had to close the bathroom door to put some distance between them, or he'd take her here and now in the hallway.

Tish regarded the closed door with amused dismay. It seemed to symbolize Mitch's approach to intimacy. He wanted her on his terms and timed so he could remain in total and daunting control. The irony of it made her smile reluctantly. That had always been her approach, too. Until Mitch.

The door opened and his arm snaked out. He dropped his soiled clothes in a heap at her feet. She smiled mischievously. He took a lot for granted, did Sheriff Connor. What did he think she was, a laundry service? Time to defend her heart a little. Grasping his hand before he could withdraw it—he'd washed it— Tish licked each soapy-tasting finger, intending to grab back the initiative Mitch was so good at stealing away from her.

It felt good. Very, very good. Gently she sucked each finger, circling it with her tongue. Her thumbs traced designs across the fleshy part of his. A little noise of pure gratification escaped her throat just as he groaned.

"Lady," came Mitch's disembodied growl, "unless you want me to make love to you through the hole in the lock, you'd better let me take my shower."

"Yes, sir, Sheriff, sir." She taunted him with a final, moist flick and she released his hand. The door shut in front of her nose with an emphatic little slam.

She made a face at the pile of clothes. Holding them away from her body, she carried his pants and shirt to Nonna's utility room and sponged the stains and perspiration marks with cold water. A few moments in the dryer had the uniform acceptable, if not in the crisp condition Mitch preferred. He'd just have to lump it. Tish felt a prickle of anxiety. Mitch carried such a burden of regrets. She wanted to give him something— herself. She wanted . . .

To love him.

Tish faced her realization unflinchingly. She calmly folded his clothes, ran up the stairs and laid his things over the back of a chair in her room. On the seat she dropped her slacks, her sleeveless blouse, then her panties and the white lace-trimmed underwire bra. The style was a compromise between prettiness and the constant battle with gravity's tug on her full, firm breasts. Looking down at herself, she fervently hoped that Mitch would like what he would see.

Wandering naked down the hallway gave her a feeling of sensual abandon. A slight, delicious wickedness. The runner felt soft and scratchy against the soles of her feet, like Mitch's beard against her palm. Her breasts swayed with a freedom she rarely allowed them.

With a complete lack of modesty—*as if I've been doing this for years,* she thought—she entered the bathroom to use the sink, washing her face and brushing her teeth, intensely aware of the shadow in the spray behind the glass shower door. She pulled a brush through her hair with long, slow strokes and wiped a circle in the condensation on the mirror.

Her face was pale. In the steam from the shower, her hair feathered into loose curls that bounced on her shoulders. Her nipples were contracted into tight, hard peaks, as if Mitch had just touched her. She looked as if she'd just come from a bed instead of being on her way to one. With Mitch. She turned longingly toward the foggy shower stall.

The door slid open. Mitch stood there, water running in rivulets over his lean muscles. Drops caught and glistened in the hairs that covered his arms and thighs. His chest was sleek and bare, with an arrow-thin line like water-darkened silk running from below his distinct pectoral muscles to the thicket of male hair below. Tish stared at Mitch wordlessly. Her whole body responded to the sight of him. She felt a moist warmth between her legs.

Mitch stepped out of the shower. "I wasn't sure you'd be here when I got out. Thought maybe I'd hallucinated everything. I—was in pretty bad shape."

"Better now?" she murmured.

"Oh, yeah." His bold gaze devoured her. "I defy a man to look at you and not feel better."

The blush started between her breasts and moved upward to her face, turning her complexion a misty honeyed-rose. Mitch let his eyes linger on the lovely color before he stared intently at her rounded breasts, her slender waist and hips, her long, long legs. He saw her tremble. He loved the way her small pink nipples tilted up, tightening again as she examined him in return.

"You'll catch cold if you don't dry off," Tish pointed out breathlessly.

"Yeah." He made no move to reach for a towel.

Moving slowly, not wanting to break the spell, Tish picked one up from the counter and stepped close to Mitch, draping the velvety terry cloth around him. With lazy, sensual movements, she rubbed his shoulders and arms and then, even more thoroughly, his hard chest. Mitch sucked in an audible breath as she sank to her knees on the bath mat to dry him farther down. His stubborn effort at control made Tish more determined to drive him past his limits. Away from his memories.

Deliberately, she nuzzled his flat belly and probed the tiny cave of his belly button with the tip of her tongue. A droplet of water remained and she licked it delicately. It was a mischievous, silly intimacy, and it had the desired effect—a sound that was part groan, part laughter, rumbled beside her ear.

Mitch's laugh choked off abruptly as she turned her attention downward. Tish hesitated, feeling him tense as he waited to see what she would do. She made a direct, frontal, loving assault. Her fingers clenched in the soft terry-cloth towel she held looped around his buttocks and she leaned forward.

At the first touch of her mouth, so light he could barely feel it, he gasped.

"Tish." His voice was thick. "Bed. Now."

She looked up with as much innocence as she could muster. "But, Mitch—"

"Now."

"Yes, Mitch." A glimpse of his belt hanging on a hook inspired her. "You go on to my room. It's the last door on the left. I'll be there in a minute."

He gripped her wrists and helped her to her feet, cradling her against him for a moment. The brief, soft, cushiony brush of her breasts dragged another groan from him. She must be shy about mentioning birth control. She should know he wouldn't object to talking about it. No one knew better than a policeman that it was better to be safe than sorry. Right now, though, he just hoped she would hurry.

"All right," he said reluctantly. "A minute."

"I promise." He left with a last glance that sent new tendrils of heat through her. She closed the door behind him and studied the gun belt with less fear than she'd expected. Maybe the overwhelming level of desire Mitch aroused in her was an antidote to her usual response. She tugged open the snap of the leather handcuff pocket without touching the revolver.

"Okay," she murmured to herself, "you can do this.

Turning with the cold metal cuffs clutched in her hand, Tish noticed the sheriff's hat perched on the shining porcelain top of the toilet tank. She tried it on for effect. The brim promptly sank to her nose. "Come on, Tish. We're trying for sultry siren, not The Three Stooges."

Pushed back far enough on her hair, the hat teetered precariously, but it did stay on. The erect posture she maintained to keep its balance gave her a model's long, sinuous stride. She made her way down the hall and stepped through her bedroom door.

Mitch lay on his side on the Madras cover, propped up on his elbow. He looked up at the scuff of her bare feet on the wooden floorboards. Tish twirled the handcuffs on her index finger. Resting her weight on one foot, she positioned her other hand saucily on her outthrust hip.

Mitch jackknifed into a sitting position, one leg straight, the other bent upward framing his arousal between them.

With the combination of nerves and desire, Tish's voice was a low purr. "Howdy, Sheriff."

Mitch's voice was hoarse. "Letizia, what are you planning to do with those?"

"These?" She dangled the cuffs enticingly. "I don't know. I thought you'd have some ideas. You said they were supposed to be a turn on." She moved closer. The hat fell to the floor and rolled away. "And, Sheriff, I really want to turn you on."

He swung his legs off the bed and stood in front of her. His rigid flesh pressed into her abdomen. Tish's ticklish, erotic waist area prickled into life, and she undulated against him, trying to feel him everywhere at once. Held loosely in her hand, the cuffs trailed across the nape of his neck.

The frantic rhythm of her hips against his almost drove Mitch past the point of sanity. He grabbed the rounded swells of her buttocks to hold her still, and buried his face in the hollow at the base of her neck, his teeth clenched with the effort not to plunge into her as they stood. She moved her hips, while her buttocks firmed and flexed in his hands.

"Honey, honey. Hold on, here."

"Okay," she said sweetly, slipping her free hand between them. "Is this what you mean? I like holding you like this."

He muttered something—a curse or a prayer—and lifted his head.

"Tish, honey, we don't need the cuffs."

"We don't?"

He was pretty sure that was relief he heard in her voice. Reaching behind him, he pulled the cuffs from her grasp and tossed them aside. They hit the dresser with a loud clink. "Absolutely not. We've both got better things to do with our hands."

"I do like the way you think." She lifted one of his hands to her mouth and teased the center of his palm with her tongue. Then she pressed the moistened palm against one of the hard nipples that tipped her full breasts.

Mitch had never felt so desperate for release in his entire life. The rapt gleam behind Tish's half-closed eyelids reassured him that she, too, was ready. "The bed," he said thickly.

"Yes. Oh, Mitch."

Mitch was closest; he fell back, taking her with him. They rolled on the narrow mattress, making breathless, urgent noises. He halted their roll before Tish could hit the wall, by chance coming to rest above her. Shudders of anticipation coursed through him as she laced her arms around his neck and wrapped her legs around his waist.

"Now, Mitch. Oh, please, now."

Mitch looked over at the nightstand. Impatiently, she tightened her thighs and lifted her hips to reinforce the invitation. "Mitch?"

"Honey, I don't see anything to protect us with. Even if you're on some kind of—"

"I'm not," she whispered. "I'm so sorry. I didn't even think about it."

Groaning, he pushed himself away from her, untangled himself from her arms and legs, and grabbed his pants. "It's okay, hon, no problem. There's a box out in the car. Just—don't forget where we were, all right?"

"You don't need to worry about that. I won't forget," she told him, laughing shakily. She felt a wave of desire when she saw the trouble he had closing the zipper. He didn't even try to fasten the button. His flat abdomen rippled as he bent and stomped to jam his feet into his boots.

"Thank you for not yelling at me." The revealing words slipped out.

Mitch merely shrugged. "Why would I yell? I should have known you wouldn't keep a stash of condoms around here." He gave her a grin that was both rueful and lascivious. "Stay right where you are. I want to see that sexy sprawl when—"

A tiny sound interrupted him. Instantly he changed from big, easy-to-be-with—and aroused—to taut, lean cautiousness. Tish smothered a gasp as he flattened himself against the doorframe, head cocked to listen.

"Expecting company?" he asked softly.

She replied in a hushed undertone. "Of course not. The grands are in San Francisco all night."

"Right. Phone up here?"

"The only phone's in the kitchen."

He swore. "Get some clothes on. Can you get out that window?"

Tish visualized the roof to the veranda and the pillars that supported it. If she couldn't shimmy down them, she might fall twenty feet. "Yes," she said without hesitation. Mitch didn't need her fear right now.

"Use the radio in my car. There's a switch on the side of the mouthpiece. Be *careful*," he ordered, and eased the tip of a boot into the hall.

"Where are you going?" she shrieked softly.

He glanced over his shoulder. "For my gun."

Heart hammering, Tish wrenched the shirt off the chair back and thrust her arms into it. The buttons seemed too large for the buttonholes. Damning her clumsy fingers, she leaned against the doorframe, straining to hear.

Despite his heavy boots, Mitch had moved in the lithe, silent crouch of a hunting animal. He made his way from the bathroom to the top of the stairs. As he passed under the ceiling light, his shadow was thrown against the wall. Tish swallowed against a bitter taste in the back of her throat at the sight of the weapon in his hand. *Predator!*

A familiar cracked laugh rang out.

"Gus," scolded Nonna's unmistakable contralto, "not so loud. Letizia must have forgotten to turn out the lights when she went to bed."

Even as she darted into the hall to warn Mitch, he was swinging the revolver's barrel harmlessly toward the ceiling. His finger eased away from the trigger. He dropped his chin to the top of her head as she hurled into him, and slid a comforting arm around her shoulders. "Hell's bells," he said with mingled relief and resignation, squeezing her gently. His bare chest felt warm and sleek under her cheek; his heartbeat slowed and settled into a solid, reassuring rhythm. Her awareness of the gun he still held kept Tish from relaxing. After a moment, she pulled away.

He followed the direction of her glance. He said calmly, "I'll put this away," and turned toward the bathroom where his gun belt hung.

"Who's up there? Letizia, are you all right?" For once, Nonna's voice was sharp. The stairs creaked.

"Oh, Lordy," Tish said, as Nonna, Pa trailing her, appeared on the landing below her.

9

THE LANDING MADE an excellent vantage point, and Tish couldn't even hope that her grandparents wouldn't notice she was naked under her shirt. Not even *her* shirt, she realized; Mitch's. The hem, thank goodness, hung almost at her knees, but in her haste she'd mismatched the few buttons and holes she'd managed to put together, so the garment gaped badly. She pulled the shirtfront together, fought the impulse to bolt, and waited while Nonna and Pa toiled determinedly up the stairs. Tish knew better than to try to stop them from attempting the climb to the landing. Although she hadn't heard him approach, Mitch's solid warmth pressed against her back. He wouldn't run and let her face the music alone, no matter how embarrassing the tune.

To her relief, neither Nonna nor Pa appeared shocked or stricken, although both raised their eyebrows.

For several excruciating moments no one said anything. Then suddenly Pa hissed and leaned forward, staring at the collar of Mitch's shirt where it gaped away from Tish's neck. Nonna's eyes widened. Tish looked helplessly from her grandparents over her shoulder to Mitch. His eyes narrowed and then lifted to hers. He spoke earnestly. "Tish, I swear I never meant to hurt you. My God—"

"Of course you haven't hurt me. There's nothing . . ." Her voice trailed away as she touched the spot at the base of her neck that seemed to concern everybody. It felt tender. "What is it?"

"I believe it's called a hickey," said Nonna. "The biggest one I've ever seen."

"Honey . . ."

As if they were alone, Mitch lifted a gentle fingertip to her neck. "I don't even remember doing that."

Suddenly Tish recalled the scrape of his teeth, just there, and felt a blush work its hot way up her neck and cheeks. "It's all right, really. I must bruise easily."

"But I knew that. You're so fragile under all that self-assurance."

Mitch seemed determined to take the blame. Tish shrugged her shoulders helplessly. "I'm okay," she lied. Everything was taking on an unnatural, crystalline shimmer, as if the hallway and the people in it would shatter at the graze of a butterfly's wing. She turned to the older couple, feeling rather desperate. "What happened? Did you decide to skip the play?"

"Not voluntarily." Nonna allowed the change of subject. "A cypress tree came down outside the Presidio tunnel. We waited a while for CalTrans trucks to haul it away, then gave up and came home."

Tish tried to concentrate. "Food. You must be starved—"

"We stopped in Marin for supper." Pa refused to be diverted. "Letizia, you're an adult now. Mitch is, too, and he's a good friend. God knows, your grandmother and I have lived a long time. That's the point. I am an old man. I am not used to coming home and finding my little girl wearing a man's shirt and bearing his mark."

His mark. The old-fashioned, un-English phrasing heightened Tish's sense of unreality. Did Mitch's mark make her Mitch's woman?

Nonsense, of course. Still, she looked up at Mitch and glimpsed an odd expression before his usual impassiveness was restored. A mixture of possessiveness, satisfaction and pain.

Mitch turned to Nonna and Pa. "You can't expect me to apologize for finding Tish attractive," he said quietly.

"No." A small smile played around Nonna's mouth. "Gus, it's late. Letizia and Mitch wish to say goodnight." She glanced meaningfully at Tish to reinforce the hint, pushed Pa through their bedroom door and shut it firmly behind them.

Mitch took a deep breath. "I guess that means I'd better be on my way."

"It would probably be best," Tish agreed, not meeting his eyes. "I'm sorry about—all this." She waved a hand that trembled slightly toward the closed door.

"Nobody's fault. They took it better than I expected. Hey—you're not worried we were doing anything wrong, are you? We're not kids taking chances."

If he touched her again, she thought, she would break into a thousand million pieces, and she didn't know what she'd look like, or feel like, or be like when she got herself put back together once more. "No," she said. "You're right. We're grown-ups taking chances. How far are we willing to go?"

He grinned wearily. "That's a hell of a question."

"I don't mean sexually. We both know that we want each other that way. I mean, are we going to try to make anything besides a—chemical attraction work between us? Are we more than a one-night stand?"

He leaned against the wall. "We haven't even been *that* yet. Close, but no cigar."

"Is that all you want? A quick lay? We can go out and do it in the back of your car," she said, so tired she wasn't shocked by the crudeness of her offer.

He put his arms around her and she discovered that she'd been wrong. She didn't break into pieces; she melted into the warmth of his chest.

"Hush," he soothed. "You don't mean that. God help us both, I do want more than a one-nighter with you. A lot more. Honey, you're falling asleep on your feet. Come on, I'll tuck you into bed."

Everything was inside out and upside down. The evening had begun with her trying to comfort him, and now he was taking care of her. Tish tried to protest as he picked her up, but the sensation of being held and carried, cradled against him and protected by his strong arms, was so lovely that the words never made it past her lips. She closed her eyes for just a moment. He placed her on the mattress and her head settled onto the pillow. She heard the covers rustle as Mitch pulled them up to her chin and felt his gentle kiss on her forehead. She tried to open her eyes to look at him; she couldn't. She heard him say, "Don't fight it, Tish, honey. Your emotions have caught up with you and worn you out. Let yourself sleep."

Of course. She was already half asleep....

AN IMPOSSIBLY STRONG smell of coffee and chocolate woke her. Tish sat up before her eyes were completely open. She blinked in the bright sunlight at Nonna, who was sitting on the edge of the bed, and was grateful that the rocks weighing down her eyelids had magically disappeared overnight.

Nonna lifted Tish's hands and closed them over a mug of steaming liquid. "Good morning, sleepyhead."

"Mocha! Mmm, it's wonderful. How do I rate the princess treatment?"

"Gus wanted me to come in and make sure you hadn't died from your hickey," Nonna said blandly.

"Oh!" Tish squinted one of her eyes closed as she peered down, trying to see the bruise, but it was a physical impossibility. She realized she was still wearing Mitch's shirt and pulled the spread up to her neck. "I seem to have survived."

"Your essential parts do look undamaged," Nonna agreed, lips twitching as she studied Tish's expression. "Are you waiting for a scolding?"

Tish inspected the creamy swirls in her cup. "I'm a little grown-up for lectures, Nonna."

"Yes. So I will say only this: You're playing with fire when you play with Mitch. I hope the fire will warm you all the rest of your life—but if you aren't careful, it's just as likely to burn you. Badly. Mitch is a virile man—"

Tish covered her face with one hand. Her shoulders shook with laughter.

"And essentially decent, as well. But men, my dear Letizia, are frequently unwilling to buy cows whose milk—"

"They get for free. Oh, Nonna, not that old cliché!"

"Sayings get repeated enough to become clichés because they're so often true," Nonna said dryly.

Tish resisted the temptation to tell Nonna that Mitch hadn't gotten anything, least of all metaphorical dairy products, from her. Besides, it might not be true much longer. She hoped. She felt a tingle of exhilaration. She loved Mitch—*Oh, Lord*, Tish thought, *I've gone and fallen in love with Mitch*—and he at least wanted more than one night of passion with her. That was enough to build on. Wasn't it?

Tish realized that the fingers of her free hand had drifted to play with the buttons of Mitch's shirt. She said, "I'll get dressed."

She returned from the bathroom wearing jeans and a peach-and-gold plaid sleeveless blouse with its collar tilted carefully up to hide the mark at the base of her throat. Nonna was standing at the window, the sash lifted so the summer smells of eucalyptus and water on dust floated into the room. Tish could hear the mixture of English and Spanish of the workers in the vineyard. "That banker didn't call last night. Come clean, Nonna. Something's going on. Are you broke?"

To her surprise, Nonna laughed. "Of course not. How could you imagine such a thing?"

Feeling rather foolish, Tish listed her suspicions. "There," said Nonna, nodding approvingly, "I told Gus you would notice. But I never thought you'd worry about our finances. The land is worth so much now. In fact, the value has gone up enough that Gus and I have considered taking out a mortgage and using the money to make an investment."

Tish pulled on canvas moccasins. "Really? You and Pa have always been so conservative with your money. Are you on to a sure thing?"

"You might say that. Our investment is you. We're starting our own winery, and we want you to be our wine maker. Gus and I will form the board of directors. You'll be chief operating officer." She produced the technical phrase with pride.

Nonna's placidly delivered bombshell made Tish sit down with a thump. "You can't be serious."

"I'm always serious."

"Baloney. You're an evil woman with a wicked sense of humor. As for your morals—that's why you didn't hit the roof when you walked in on Mitch and me. He's—he's bait. You want me involved with somebody from around here so I'll come home to stay. Admit it!"

"Of course, Gus and I want you near us," Nonna said calmly. "You're the light of our lives, Letizia."

Tears threatened, and Tish abandoned her teasing tone. "Oh, Nonna. I love you, I do. But you must know I can't let you and Pa risk everything to help me start a business. The failure rate for new wineries—"

"You won't fail."

At the simple faith in her grandmother's statement, the tears fell. Tish wiped them away with an impatient hand. "I'm good at making wine. But I'm not as brilliant as all that. Hundreds of business decisions go into launching a successful venture. How do you know I'm up to it?"

"What do you do when you return to your dreadful little apartment after working all day for that conglomerate that sells swill for five dollars a bottle?"

Tish sighed. "Study business manuals."

"Why?"

"All right. So I'll be able to make solid decisions when I have enough saved to buy into a winery. But that's *my* dream, not yours. I'm not going to let you—"

"What makes you think you know every one of our dreams—Gus's and mine?" asked Nonna fiercely. "We've grown grapes on this land for almost twice as long as you've been alive, young lady. Superior grapes. And we've sold them, year after year, for the best price we could get, sometimes to companies so bad you could swear the stink of their plastic bottle caps clung to the check. And each year at harvest time, we talked about some day when we would use our own grapes to make our own vintages. 'Some day' is here. Now. We can make it happen together."

Tish wavered until she looked up and met Nonna's unblinking gaze. Deep in thought, Tish picked up a peach-colored elasticized band from the dresser and pulled her hair back into a ponytail. "You ought to be in politics. You almost had me convinced there."

"What is it you're afraid of?"

"That you'll talk me into going along with you," Tish admitted frankly. "This place is all you have. I'm sorry, but I'm not obsessed enough with the idea of being my own boss and making my own wines to encourage you to mortgage all you own at this time in your life. It's sweet of you—"

Nonna waved her thanks away. "What else are you afraid of?"

"Well—well, it took me months to get the crummy job I have now. Jonathan knows everybody in the wine business and he called all his buddies. I'm blacklisted. The only reason I got hired at all is that I'm so far down on the totem pole, nobody's noticed me. What if we go into business and we fail big? That'll be it. I'll never work in the wine industry again, at any level." Tish observed her grandmother's response carefully.

Nonna was skeptical. "I saw you for the first time when you were an hour old, red and tiny and trying to escape from your blanket. Are you saying you've turned into a coward since then? I don't believe you."

Tish turned her palms up in surrender and grinned. "I thought I'd try applying some guilt. Won't work, huh?"

"Not with me. I've had two children and eleven grandchildren and thirteen great-grandchildren. I've forgotten more about how to apply guilt than you'll ever learn. You're too tenderhearted. And I'm not going to let you change the subject yet. Listen. Gus and I have thought this out with great care. The bank is very cooperative—"

"I'll just bet," muttered Tish, thinking of the glee with which any bank would foreclose on her grandparents' prime chunk of California real estate.

Nonna named a sum almost ten times Tish's carefully hoarded savings. "That's what Mr. French said we could borrow."

"And how much of your property would stand as collateral?" Tish asked grimly.

"All of it."

Tish was shocked. "You and Pa would gamble even the house on me?"

Nonna tsked gently. "Not a gamble, dearest. A sure thing. For you, too. And in our wills, we'll make sure you reap the benefits of your work. Complete control of the winery. Also half the property—your father's share if he had lived. The other half to Aurelia and her heirs."

"That's not really fair. There are a lot more of them than there are of me," Tish argued. "They'll feel awful if you leave such a big part of the estate to one person. For Pete's sake, they'll think you don't care for them."

"Not one of your cousins has your love for the grapes or the feel for making wine." Nonna declared. She held up a hand to stop Tish's rebuttal. "If you decide any of *their* children has the talent, you can always take one or more of them into the business with you. Gus and I aren't worried about you doing the right thing. We know you will."

"Oh, stop talking as if you had one foot in the grave," said Tish, hiding very real fear under her asperity. When had her grandparents decided they were old? During the past year, when Tish had been so busy setting up her own life.... Perhaps she should consider relocating to Sonoma County. But what would she do for a job? She certainly couldn't fall in with this fuzzy-minded plan of Nonna and Pa's.

"Eucalyptus Creek."

"What about it?"

"That's the name we've chosen. Eucalyptus Creek. Remember the stone barn by the creek in the west field? It's near the highway exit. We could put the equipment and tasting room there and build on when it's time to

expand. The barn and creek can go on the label. 'Picturesque' sells."

Not so fuzzy-minded, after all. Still... "Nonna, this
is nuts. Promise me you won't sign any papers with the
bank behind my back."

"Really, Letizia—"

"Promise."

"I can't make any promises." Nonna held up a hand.
"But Mr. French is very accommodating. We can wait
to talk until you decide to join us."

Tish needed time to think this over. "Can I borrow
the car to go to town?"

Sonoma wasn't much more than a village but it did
have public phones. A few weeks ago she wouldn't have
believed anything would take priority in her life over
ambition, but the urge to hear Mitch's voice was almost an ache.

Nonna hesitated. "I see no reason why not. As long
as you're home by one-thirty," she added.

"Okay," said Tish. "I suppose there's no point in
asking if you or Pa could drive me to the hall? I could
pick up my car and the two of you would have
yours...."

"We wouldn't be able to make it out and back in time
because some friends are dropping by. They are looking forward to seeing you," Nonna told her firmly.

Tish rolled her eyes. "Right. I'll be here at one-thirty."

SONOMA HAD GROWN, she noted as she turned on to the
long, straight road that led through the business dis-
trict to the town square. The square remained a reassuring tribute to the commercial potential of nostalgia.

It was surrounded by two and three-story buildings—some dating from the Depression, others old, charming adobe with timbered balconies. Families of ducks still waddled in and out of marshy pools in the park. Down a side street stood the quiet refuge of Mission San Francisco de Solano. Tourists in shorts and sunglasses sauntered everywhere.

Tish eased into a parking spot and found a phone nearby. She wished for the semiprivacy of a booth instead of the freestanding shell and then decided she was being silly. None of the strangers idling around her cared about what she had to say. Fabulous odors were wafting from the bakery a few doors down. When she finished her call, that bakery could use some serious investigation.

After a quick check of the phone book, she realized that Mitch's home number was unlisted. *Well, of course*, she derided herself. He'd never get any sleep otherwise, between the kooks and the criminals. A long-distance call to Santa Rosa, the county seat, garnered scant information from the receptionist. The sheriff wasn't in. It was impossible to say for certain when the sheriff would be in. The sheriff's address and phone number were confidential information. A message would be delivered promptly in case of emergency.

"No, it's not an emergency," Tish admitted. *Except to me*.

She hung up. Love was the pits. She'd always known that it brought a pounding heart, sweaty palms, fierce elation and even fiercer loneliness.

Who needed it?

10

ALTHOUGH SHE'D LOST her appetite, Tish stood in line
for a loaf of sourdough bread. Trying to decide what
her grandparents might like with it, she dawdled
through the square, ending up on the opposite side at
the entrance to a cheese factory. The deli section was
open and crowded with customers.

Tish waited impatiently in another line until she
could pay for a wedge of Sonoma jack. Accepting her
change, she turned and bumped into a solid male chest.

"Mitch!"

He caught her by the elbows and steadied her. "Hi."

Her heart began to pound. Love might be a terrible
invention but, oh, Mitch looked good. "I was trying to
call you."

"I'm flattered. My number's not listed."

"I found that out. Do you have time to talk?" He wore
a Western-cut shirt and well-worn jeans.

"This'll probably strike you as an incredible coincidence. I wanted to talk to you, too." He nodded toward a redwood picnic table on the deli's flower-decked
patio, and continued to hold her elbow until she maneuvered herself and her bags of food onto a bench.
"Hungry?"

Suddenly she was ravenous. "Yes, please. A sandwich, anything."

He was back much sooner than she'd expected. "What did you do, take cuts?" she teased as she peeked inside the French roll. Pink roast beef with avocado and a thick slab of the same jack she'd just bought. She took an enthusiastic bite.

"Taking cuts would be dishonest," Mitch replied, sitting down beside her. "There was a momentary lull in business." At her skeptical glance, he grinned. "It could be the girl behind the counter thought I was cute. She told me she gets off at five."

Tish licked a dab of mayonnaise from the side of her roll. "You are cute. Are you going to meet her?"

Mitch's wiry brows rose. "I hadn't considered it. I was assuming—hoping—you'd object. Was I wrong?"

"You know how to put somebody on the spot, don't you?" she answered wryly. She put down her sandwich. "Mitch, what do you want out of a relationship?"

Sun filtered down through the trellised roof, laying bars of light across his face as he spoke. "I thought about this a lot last night after I went home. You're not very conducive to sleep, you know. If you'd asked me two weeks ago, I would have said I didn't want a relationship at all. I got pretty burned while I was married."

"I thought," Tish ventured carefully, "I thought from what you said before, that you were close to your wife."

"Close? No. We had sort of an on-and-off infatuation. I was nuts about her but I couldn't live with the way she ran around." He shrugged. "Carol claimed to be nuts about me, too, and said she went with other guys only because she couldn't stand the hours I had to work or the—suspense, I guess—not knowing from one day to the next if I'd get blown away. She'd go trolling for pickups in bars."

"A perfect revenge on a proud man," Tish whispered, appalled. Mitch had said his mother had sold her body to men she found in bars. She wondered if Carol had known how complete the revenge must have been.

Mitch spoke matter-of-factly. "We tried a separation; it didn't last long. She called, crying, and— Hell, she was my wife so I took her back. We really tried to make it work. The baby coming helped. She was into fidelity right then, and I knew the baby was mine. Maybe becoming parents wouldn't have made a difference in the long run. I know experts say a bad marriage can't be saved by having a child, but it was our last chance."

Mitch wasn't eating, either. Tish linked fingers with him and they sat quietly.

Mitch stirred and picked up his bread-and-butter pickle. "Common sense isn't the main requirement for getting involved."

"Are we talking about the past or the present?" she asked without looking at him.

"What do you think?"

She traced the carved initials intertwined in a heart on the soft redwood table. *Getting involved.* Not *falling in love.* "It's quite a coincidence, you finding me in town today."

The sun made little auburn highlights in his hair that zigzagged as he shook his head. "Not exactly. I wasn't sure what the situation would be at Gus and Magda's, so I got the cops on patrol to keep their eyes peeled. You were spotted the minute you hit Highway 12. Female, Caucasian, twenty-nine, brunette, brown eyes. No distinguishing marks except that you're astonishingly pretty. I like the ponytail. You were driving a tan Plymouth coupe, license number—"

Her shocked stare caught him by surprise. "You're having me watched?"

"That's kind of a dramatic way to put it. A couple of brother officers did me a favor, that's all."

"How nice," she said scathingly. "How delightful that you have—have surveillance capabilities at your fingertips. Is that how you found out Carol was having affairs? You had her watched?"

Mitch felt some of the old anger twist and roil. He'd kept it curbed for more years than he could remember. "No, I didn't. She was only too glad to tell me whenever she found some substitute. It was all part of the game with her. She got the sex and the excitement of sneaking around places she knew I didn't want her in, and my attention to boot. What game are we playing now, Tish? Why are you mad?"

Shame sent heat into her cheeks. The hell Mitch had lived through trying to honor his wedding vows had been worse than her own. She owed him an explanation.

"It's not the first time I've been followed." Her voice was dull. "My ex-husband kept detectives on me most of the time I was married to him. Seven years."

Mitch didn't say anything. Despite the fact that they were in a public place, he jerked the bench away from the table and pulled her roughly into his lap, stroking her hair over and over again.

"He must have felt guilty," she continued. "His moral code was weird. Something out of the Dark Ages. I mean, he slept with every female employee his companies hired. *Droit de seigneur* or something. But me, I was his property and, by God, I'd better remember to act that way." She lifted her eyes to meet his bleak gaze. "I was never unfaithful. Wouldn't have been even if I'd had the chance. Maybe he had to imagine I was just like him to justify the way he behaved."

"When did you find out?"

"One of his more naive secretaries fell for him and then found out she was only one in a long line. She was outraged that her lover had other mistresses, so she let me in on the secret, too. Poor thing, she must have thought I was deranged. I danced around the room, I was so happy. It was an excuse to break free, you see."

"Why'd you stay with him so long?"

"Inertia, I guess." Tish gestured with her hands as she tried to shape her thoughts. "Fear of loss. Some parts of my life were very comfortable. The gilded-cage syndrome. And nobody in my family had ever been divorced before. I know it sounds ridiculous in this day and age, but I was ashamed. And scared."

"Did he threaten you? Abuse you?" Mitch asked abruptly.

The truth trembled on her tongue and she bit it back. Some things were better not discussed, even with Mitch. Maybe especially with Mitch, who packed a gun as if it were part of his body. "He never hit me," she said honestly. "And he definitely didn't rape me. In fact, he hardly ever touched me."

Mitch was flatteringly incredulous. "Was he insane? To pick a string of bimbos over you?"

Laughter eased some of Tish's tension. "No doubt. Don't you think we'd better be going? There are people waiting for a table."

Carrying her bags, Mitch hesitated as they passed through the wine section. Tish had been eyeing the labels surreptitiously to get an idea what was selling without forcing him to linger. She waited uncertainly, and read a notice posted on the side of a rack.

She gasped in delight. "Henri Tericot is speaking tonight and it's open to the public!"

"Should I be thrilled? Who is this guy?"

"Just one of the top wine experts in the world. He really knows his stuff. I don't suppose you'd want to come with me to hear him?" She looked at him without much hope.

He smiled crookedly. "I'll pass. But look at this."

Tish took the bottle from his hand. "Nonalcoholic wine? Ever tried it?"

"Can't say that I have."

"Opinions vary of course, but generally it doesn't have a very good reputation. No complexity, no fullness. Sort of a fringe thing in the wine world."

"Still, it ought to be appealing to folks who shouldn't drink the harder stuff."

"Read the small print. It contains alcohol. Not much, but some. Toxic for recovering alcoholics. You probably know better than I do that the only treatment for alcoholism is avoiding alcohol altogether."

"Yeah." He looked at her quizzically. "I'm surprised to hear you say it, though."

Tish put the bottle back in its rack. "You don't believe anybody has a social conscience except you."

He smiled. "Not true. But I didn't expect a wine maker to advocate abolishing alcohol."

"Give me a break, Sheriff. That's not what I said. You can't close all the wineries because some people can't drink, any more than you could shut down the drug companies because some people react badly to penicillin. Prohibition didn't work, remember?"

Swinging open the door to the sidewalk, Mitch didn't answer. Tish went on aggressively. "There's something you should know if we're going to *get involved*." She told him about her grandparents' plan to borrow against their property. "It's really wonderful of them to want to do it," she added, "and I'm incredibly flattered by their belief in me. But, Lord, the risk they'd be taking! Not to mention the time component—at least a year just to get the equipment in place and then waiting for a harvest. And wine doesn't mature overnight, you know. It would take us four or five years to get the first inkling of whether or not I'd managed us into bankruptcy."

"Sounds like a risky sort of venture for all of you," Mitch said, without heat but also without encouragement.

Tish smiled at his effort at neutrality. His grim expression softened.

"Oh, I've got some money I'd toss into the pot," she said. "I've been practicing all sorts of economies to save for just this kind of opportunity."

Mitch nodded in sudden comprehension. "That junk heap you drive."

"It runs," she pointed out defensively.

"Honey, I'm not knocking it. I'd lock you up before I'd let you behind the wheel of a really powerful car." She glared at him and he grinned. "You look good in plastic pearls."

She couldn't help but laugh. It seemed a very long week ago since she'd agonized over whether anyone would guess she was no long wearing the real thing. "Then I'd better cultivate a taste for dime-store jewelry. If I were to go bananas along with Nonna and Pa, it would be quite a while before we'd see a profit for splurging on luxuries."

The reflective tone of her voice prodded Mitch's private demons. She wanted to make wine; she yearned for the chance. If this thing with her grandparents didn't pan out, she'd find another winery to invest in and work to promote it with all her intelligence and enthusiasm. He knew his viewpoint was extreme, but that failed to alter the sick feeling in his stomach.

"Hey." Using his free arm, he caught her around the waist as she was about to step off the curb. A horn honked. She ignored it and relaxed into his embrace with a trusting snuggle. Just the right size, he thought, jolted again by the knowledge. It seemed vitally important, all of a sudden. Just the right fit. Her breasts pressed into his side.

"Hey, what?"

He rubbed his chin against her hair. "Hey, want to come over to my place for a while?"

"For how long?"

"Long enough, I hope." He shifted his grip so their bodies dovetailed perfectly, as if sliding into predestined slots; face-to-face, chest to breast, hips molding together, thighs in erotic conjunction.

"Mitch, I can't. I promised Nonna I'd be home at one-thirty. It's nearly that now. She's got some friends dropping by who expect to see me."

Grimacing, he released her. "I'd better let you go, then, or it'll be pretty embarrassing to walk around in public."

They dashed across the traffic that circled the park. A few steps into the green space and the squeal of tires and haze of auto exhaust faded away as if by magic, held at bay by fragrant evergreens.

Mitch set her bags in the back seat when they reached the D'Angeli car. "Where's your vehicle?"

"Mitch, regular people don't say 'vehicle.' Did you learn that at the police academy?"

"No, from old episodes of *Adam-12.* Is yours out of commission?"

Tish fluttered her hands in an old-world gesture she must have picked up from her family. Mitch liked it. It bespoke roots that went deep. "Parked at the hall where Nonna and Pa had their reception." She sighed.

"Still? We could run out and pick it up later. And then maybe do some other things together."

"What kinds of things?"

"I'm sure we could think of something."

"Sounds very nice. After the lecture, then?"

"Oh. Yeah." His lips lost their lazy curve and tightened into a straight line. "Your Monsieur what's-his-name."

Tish looked at him steadily. He wasn't sure where he got the impression that she had to force herself not to shrink away from him. "Is the fact I want to attend Tericot's speech a problem for you? I can skip it."

"Don't be ridiculous. Of course you should go. I've—got some reading to catch up on tonight. I'll call you tomorrow."

Tish stood tall and proud and very, very defensive. "Or I could call you."

"Whatever you like."

Slamming the door, Tish whipped the coupe out of the parking place as if she were revving for a demolition derby, vehemently telling herself that she didn't care if he liked the way she drove or not.

She slowed as she joined the flow of traffic. The volume of cars was too heavy for idiotic bravado behind the wheel. Besides, she didn't trust Mitch not to call the town police and turn her in for reckless driving.

Her anger ebbed as excitement filled her. They were going to be lovers.... How stupid to let a disagreement about a lecture keep her from becoming Mitch's lover as soon as possible. Would he be standing on the sidewalk if she pulled a U-turn and went back?

Only her promise to Nonna kept Tish going east toward her grandparents' house. Oddly enough, euphoria cleared her thinking. She'd forgotten to get Mitch's phone number but surely it would be listed in Nonna's address book. She'd call Mitch when she got to the house; her normal need for privacy from her relatives' too-curious ears wouldn't stand in her way.

She drove on, senses alive to the clean summer smells and the glints of gold and purple in the grasses waving in the ditches by the side of the road. The hills rose and fell before her. *Home,* she thought happily.

Several cars were parked in the circular driveway. None looked familiar, but she knew everyone who came spilling off the porch—Nonna and Pa, Belle and her Frank, their children, Mr. Fontana... Heavens! Aunt Aurelia, actually smiling?

"What's the occasion?" she asked, shutting the garage door.

"Surprise! Surprise! See your car? Look what Mr. Fontana did!"

The boys surrounded her, tugging on her pockets and pulling out her shirttails in an effort to push her toward a pristine subcompact, its buffed black surface and showy chrome shining in the sun.

"That's not my car," Tish said with conviction.

"Yes, it is! Yes, it is!"

Mr. Fontana called out to her as she circled the vehicle, impelled by the enthusiastic youngsters. "We couldn't match the blue for you. Well, the factory doesn't make it anymore. So we went with black. The interior was no problem, so long as you like white...."

It was impossible to tell where dents had marred the now smooth frame, and the stark black, white and silver color scheme elevated its boxy shape to something like elegance. Tish turned and threw her arms around her grandfather's old friend. "You're a magician. How did you make the old wreck look so good?"

He patted her awkwardly. "A little paint, a few scraps of material, a tap with the hammer here and there. An afternoon's work. A bagatelle. Just tell me you like it."

"Of course I like it! You'll let me pay—"

He gave her a little shake and let her go. "None of that kind of talk. Don't insult an old man whose happiness is to see you happy. It was nothing."

His "nothing" included two brand-new bumpers, at least one new fender and a sunroof, which she'd never had before. This major renovation job must be worth thousands of dollars. He'd probably overhauled the engine, too; she wouldn't put it past him. The stubborn set to his jaw stopped her from protesting further.

"I can't ever thank you enough for such a magnificent gift."

He smiled. "Enjoy it. That's thanks enough."

While Belle's sons pestered him with questions about the sunroof, the other relatives surged forward. When the excited laughter and affectionate chatter calmed, Tish sat cross-legged on the lawn beside Belle. She accepted a beer from Frank and spoke freely about the budget she'd imposed on herself for the past year.

Belle gave them a hilarious rundown on the costs of raising children in the video-game age. As she laughed, Tish felt the last bit of defensive caution ease and drift away. Her loss of income didn't matter to these people. Not one of them judged her for a failed marriage or losing the Keller millions.

Tish drew a design in the condensation on her can. "There's something else I have to talk to you about. Not here."

Belle looked up from diapering her youngest child. "Want to go to the beach tomorrow? I'll get a sitter for little Gus and we can make an afternoon of it."

"That would be fun. It's been forever since I've been to the beach."

Taking advantage of her moment of inattention, little Gus chortled and rolled out of Belle's grasp. He tumbled onto chubby hands and knees, thrust himself up on hands and feet, then pushed himself upright and stumbled away on unsteady legs, his bare bottom eliciting joking catcalls.

Tish ran after him and picked him up in a bear hug, twirling around happily. He laughed and leaned against her chest. The trusting motion made her disconcertingly aware that breasts existed for nurturing as well as pleasure. The baby smells of powder, scented wipes and milk filled her nostrils. The intimacy of his incredibly soft skin and his naked bottom against her bare inner arms evoked instincts she'd never been aware of. She stopped in her tracks. Twenty-nine wasn't so old to start having babies these days.

Did Mitch like babies? He'd wanted one with his late wife—cement to hold their disintegrating marriage together. But did he like them, as well? Demanding, time-consuming, lovable babies . . . Tish didn't know.

"You'd better let me get a diaper on him or you're going to get christened," Belle said prosaically. Tish handed the child over, wondering at her impulses. Motherhood had never been one of her priorities. Other goals had always taken precedence, but suddenly the most important question in the world was whether the children she gave Mitch might have a chance of inheriting his coloring. . . .

And he hadn't given her any indication at all that he wanted more than a pleasantly selfish, childless relationship limited to the emotional limits of getting involved.

LATER IN THE DAY, all the relatives gathered around as Tish got into her beautiful refinished car and switched on the ignition. The children clapped enthusiastically as the engine purred smoothly, and she waved happily as she drove off. It ran like a top, like a completely different machine, all the way into Sonoma. Every once in a while she stroked the new upholstery. She was touched by Mr. Fontana's generosity.

Entering the auditorium alone, she was very aware that Mitch wasn't with her for Henri Tericot's lecture. How many things was "getting involved" going to exclude? Babies? Companionable evenings? Would she and Mitch be lovers but never the kind of friends who understood each other's interests?

She sat in a folding chair near the front, her expression one of intelligent attention. Mr. Tericot spoke with passion and authority about a subject she'd always found fascinating.

She didn't hear a word he said.

11

TISH DARED 101 the next morning in her refurbished car.
Santa Rosa had changed, too, she thought. In fact, if it
hadn't been for the highway exit signs, she wouldn't
have been able to tell where the town limits began and
the surrounding townships ended. They used to be
separate entities, each with a charming and distinct
personality of its own. Now the highway snaked
through a corridor of tract homes and indistinguish-
able, stapled-together warehouses and office buildings, all new and some attractive. Tish broke out in a
cold sweat. If Nonna and Pa mortgaged their land and
Eucalyptus Creek Winery failed to turn a profit, they
could lose their vineyards to the same kind of development.

Downtown Santa Rosa had been so gentrified that it
was almost unrecognizable. She drove down a familiar street before a sharply veering car and a cacophony
of honking horns informed her that the street had become one-way. Hoping fate would keep Mitch from
finding out about her error, she parked half a mile from
the county office building and walked. Better safe than
sorry. His opinion of her driving already hovered
somewhere below abysmal. She didn't want to give him
ammunition for any more wisecracks.

The big white building seemed to waver behind a film of heat waves. She was sent from receptionist to receptionist until finally she repeated her request to a blonde with an appealing face. "I was hoping to speak to the sheriff."

The blonde studied Tish's pale gold oversize T-shirt, her rolled sleeves and matching slim skirt before fixing bright blue eyes on her face. "I'm sorry, he's not in." Her formality didn't match the gleam of curiosity in her eyes. "May I help you?"

"Uh, no. If he's not here . . . It's just that I keep getting his answering machine at home. I'll try to reach him at that number again. Thanks, anyway."

"Wait." The blonde bounced out of her chair. "I'm Suzie Simmons, Mitch's secretary."

"Tish D'Angeli."

"Hey, I recognize you! I was a couple of years behind you in school. I remember when you got married. You're unmarried now? And you're the reason Mitch has been in such a swivet lately, right? Am I right?"

Tish said cautiously, "I'm not sure what you mean."

Suzie clucked. "Listen, when Mitch Connor, cop of iron, actually takes a vacation day and forgets his big crusade cruising around looking for bad guys—"

"I don't understand. I thought patrolling was part of his job. He's on vacation?"

"That's what he calls it, although he's been working a full shift with the deputies. He just uses his vacation to escape the paperwork for a while. But that's what I'm saying. He forgot to report in last night. And he called in today and said he'd be out of town till tomorrow. So, are you tight with Mitch?"

"Apparently not," Tish said, feeling rather dazed. "He didn't tell me he was going out of town."

Suzie waved the conclusion away. "He wouldn't have told me except I need to know for the office. Irritating, isn't he? It's a shame he's not ambitious enough for me—I could really have gone for him."

Tish felt an instant, protective surge of pride in Mitch's accomplishments. She said stiffly, "Being sheriff in a large county like this one seems pretty important to me."

"Oh, it's okay if you're not looking for something better," Suzie said airily. Tish realized with some amusement that the other woman was giving her the go-ahead with Mitch. A generous sort, Mitch's secretary, in a strange kind of way. "I have high standards. I used to want someone who was young, handsome and rich. Now basically I'm in the market for a man who's under ninety and can breathe without an oxygen tent. He still has to be rich, though. Filthy rich." Consternation crossed the round face. "Oh, no," she moaned. "I forgot. You, uh, you—"

"I married filthy rich myself," Tish admitted. "It didn't work out. Be careful what you want. You might get it."

Suzie grinned and shook out her fluffy curls. "I intend to. But don't worry about me. Mitch takes me out sometimes because I'm sort of a convenience—you know, to boring dinners and things. We're just friends. Are you serious about him?"

"I really haven't known him that long," replied Tish. Suzie's direct approach left her feeling battered.

"He grows on you." Suzie laughed. "Listen to me. I sound like his sister trying to hustle him a date or something. The last thing in the world he needs is a matchmaker. I mean, is the man sexy or what?"

Tish studied the floor. How she felt about Mitch was new and precious, and given the fact that Mitch had never mentioned his feelings at all, she decided with sudden determination that she didn't want to discuss him with anyone. Not Suzie, not Belle, not Nonna.

She looked up. "Could I leave a message for him?"

"Well." Suzie's confiding air faded a trifle. "Sure."

Tish scrawled a few lines telling Mitch that she'd be at the stone barn in the west field at noon the next day. She hesitated over the signature and then scribbled, "Love, Letizia." The common closing for a note; only she had to know she meant it literally.

It wasn't until she'd parked at the beach that it occurred to her she'd signed the name Mitch preferred. Her own, real name.

Belle was already stretched out in a beach chair. The fluorescent orange stripes of her bathing suit glowed in the sunlight sifting through the sequoias bordering the riverbank.

"Bless you," said Tish, sinking into a matching chair. She shucked her outer garments to reveal a forties-inspired, scarlet two-piece swimsuit. She dug her toes in the sand. The Russian River tumbled by with a muted roar. "This is perfect. Where are all the people?"

"The gays hang out up there." Belle pointed toward a bend in the waterway. "And the nudists camp at that end."

Tish leaned forward. "Rats, I can't see anything through the trees."

They both burst into giggles. Belle passed her a container of yogurt. "You said that's what you eat."

Tish took it with a distinct lack of enthusiasm. "I did, didn't I? It's certainly time I started watching what I put in my stomach—and on my hips. I've been pigging out. Nonna's cooked all her special dishes."

"She's always been like a mother hen with one chick with you," Belle said without resentment.

"Do you think so?" Tish asked worriedly. She let the spoon plop back into the creamy stuff. "That's what I need to talk to you about. Nonna and Pa have this plan...."

With her gaze straying over the gray-green water, her cousin listened, saying tranquilly at the end of Tish's recital, "Sure. The whole family knows about Eucalyptus Creek."

"Don't you understand? They intend to will me half of everything, plus control of the business. What's the matter with you? Why aren't you mad?"

"Well, horsepucky, Tish, I don't want to run a winery. Neither do any of my brothers or sisters. You're welcome to the headaches. As for the property, let's face it. It's only worth cold, hard cash if we sell it. Nobody wants to do that—it's our heritage. We know you can make a go of pressing wine from our own grapes, and then at least the land will stay in the family. We'll all have a share in it."

Tears burned behind Tish's eyelids. "Thanks for the vote of confidence, but— Oh, Belle, I'm so scared. I could lose everything for everybody. The bank could end up with all of it."

"Try to remember you're the smart cousin," Belle admonished.

"If I'm so smart, why can't I decide what to do?" she asked, blinking hard. "Tell me that."

"Search me. There's another thing. The grands were both awfully sick a couple of months ago. Nothing serious, just Pa's eyesight and Nonna's circulation, but the horrible part was they weren't getting any better even though the doctor said they should. They just sat around moping and—and getting old right in front of our eyes. Then one day Pa was rambling on about how they'd always wanted to own their own winery, and all of a sudden they were bright-eyed and bushy tailed and plotting how to—" Belle stopped.

Tish smiled wryly. "Let me guess. How to get me to come home and stay put."

Belle made shooing motions at a persistent jay that was dive-bombing to investigate their yogurt cartons. The bird shot away with a flash of vivid blue wings and a raucous caw. "I love your bathing suit. It makes you look like an Italian movie star."

Tish accepted the change of subject. "Yours is pretty hot, too. Oh, look! There really is a nudist camp down there!"

"Want to wander on over?"

Rolling her eyes at Belle's naughty grin, Tish said, "No, thanks. You go ahead if you want." She peeked again. None of the male bodies she glimpsed down the river affected her the way Mitch's did. Not that she would have joined them in any case, but her lack of response—of interest, even—confirmed what she already knew beyond any doubt: Mitch was special.

"Are you kidding?" Belle scoffed. "This suit has extra-firm support. There's no way I'm taking it off to let gravity do its dirty work on my figure. Those itty-bitty girls can run around nude and not worry about their chests bouncing down around their knees."

Tish eyed her analytically. "I think we've both got a few good years ahead of us before the, uh, worst happens."

"Laugh all you want. I've got to protect Frank's investment in marital bliss. It's easy for you, you don't know how you have to fight to keep your shape after the kids start coming— Oh, Tish, my big mouth. Did I say the wrong thing? Have you had a yen for a baby all these years?"

"No." Sitting up, Tish wrapped her arms around her legs and rested her cheek on her knees. "Not that long. Lately, though . . . I guess my biological clock is ticking."

"Biological clock or biological urges?" Belle asked shrewdly. "Did you begin thinking about babies before you met Mitch?"

"Not really," Tish admitted.

"Right. You know, he's—"

"Oh, please. No more lectures on how he's God's gift to the sexually deprived. I can tell he is, for Pete's sake!"

"So what's stopping you from going after him?" Belle demanded.

Tish sighed. "He's out of town."

DEW HAD GATHERED in perfect crystal drops on the rose petals when Tish let herself out the kitchen door. The brilliant red roses and moist, fresh air seduced her. She dropped the basket that she had looped over one arm, plucked a half-opened, sweetly scented bud and clipped it into her hair with a barrette. The rose matched her sleeveless top and shorts, adding a festive touch. Feeling fresh and alive, she picked up the basket and went to her car.

It was early, but Tish had already been up for an hour frying chicken and assembling potato salad for a picnic. Savory odors filled the car seat. She patted the basket's wooden lid as she steered over the winding track leading to the stone barn. Pa had asked her to check it over as a possible site for Eucalyptus Creek Winery. "Not that I'm won over," she'd warned him, but Pa had just winked solemnly at Nonna while he assured Tish that no one meant to put any pressure on her.

"Sure," she muttered to herself. She parked the car a little distance from the barn, behind a rise, so she could approach it on foot and gauge its picturesque qualities—and structural deficiencies—for herself.

The gray stone structure, roofed in blue tile, loomed up out of the field. Under the morning cloud cover the building looked cool and sturdy and very large. Almost large enough, Tish grudgingly admitted to herself. Pushing her way through a stand of milkweed, she rounded a corner and stopped, stunned.

Someone had been very busy.

"Pa-a-a!" Her wail bounced off the stone wall and echoed back at her.

An entire new wing had been added to the barn. It would be invisible from customers who'd happily pay extra for charm with their wine but who might balk at premium prices for a luxury product developed in a plain, functional prefab. Wildly estimating how much her grandparents had already sunk into the building, Tish fumbled through the ring of keys Pa had given her the night before until she found one that fit the lock in the new door.

Inside, she gave the place one comprehensive glance. It was stacked to the ceiling with cartons. She'd have a lot to do if she accepted the project. Muttering under her breath, she unearthed a pad and pencil from her purse and settled down to draft preliminary plans for the winery.

Three hours later, Tish was taking a break in the barn, leaning her shoulder against a wooden barrel and tracing the intricate carving with an appreciative finger when she felt a prickling at the back of her neck. She whirled around.

"Hi. You should never leave a door unlocked."

My lover, she thought. Then, *My not-quite lover*. Mitch wore well-washed jeans and another Western shirt, this one with sleeves rolled up to reveal muscular arms. "Hello. I guess I just forgot about locking up behind me. This place is kind of overwhelming."

Mitch tipped back his sandy head and gave the cavernous room a once-over from ceiling to floor. His tone remained politely unimpressed. "Yeah?"

She rapped on the ten-foot-tall barrel beside her. "French oak. Absolutely perfect condition. Capacity—about a thousand gallons. There are dozens of them, hand turned and hand carved with harvest scenes. Pa must have looted them from a vintner going out of business. The tourists will love them. Go back into the addition. The vats in there are aluminum, finest quality. There's enough first-class chemistry equipment to build my own atom bomb, all of it brand-new and still in the shipping cases."

"Gus and Magda aren't waiting for you to make up your mind," said Mitch slowly.

"It doesn't look like it, no," she agreed. "A month or two to set up, some grapes to press and this could be a working winery. Where did they get the money? Nonna swore they haven't signed the mortgage papers yet! At least," she added doubtfully, "I think she did."

"Magda can be pretty slippery when she's doing something for your own good. Or what she's decided is for your own good. What exactly did she say?"

"I can't remember. Something vague about what the loan officer at the bank had promised. Mitch, hundreds of thousands of dollars have been sunk into this place already. What am I going to do?"

"We could eat," he suggested with a crooked smile.

"I suppose." Sighing, she put her hands to her hair, and discovered the rosebud behind her ear. "Oh, I forgot this poor thing. It must be wilted by now."

"I'll take care of it." Mitch came close to unhook the barrette.

"Are you still mad?" she asked.

"Nope. You?"

"No."

As his big fingers worked delicately to free the clip and flower from several stubborn strands of her hair,

Tish felt small and fragile, as if in a moment she might be crushed between the huge barrel behind her and the tall man standing within kissing distance. His broad shoulders blocked her view of the room. They blocked out everything—the world, the past, the need to breathe and especially the reasons to think.... As the loosened ornaments slipped from her hair, she stood on tiptoe to kiss him.

He let her lips explore, his closed lips remaining pliant under the moving warmth of her mouth. When her tongue glided out to gain entrance, he took control, pressing forward, rubbing his lips against hers with a gentle authority that made it clear he wasn't going to allow her to deepen the caress.

He broke the contact. But even though he stepped back, the hunger in his eyes reminded her of shaded lamplight and shared desire, and the undeniable fact that they needed only each other to create excitement in their lovemaking. "Mitch..." The whispered name was both a plea and a demand.

He trailed the rosebud across her cheek. "Listen, lady, I've been thinking about some of the things you've said to me, and I'm not giving you a chance to decide I'm some animal that can't raise its mind above sex. We're going to do this right. I'm going to prove to you I didn't come here today just to take advantage of your tempting body."

"Willing body," she corrected, trailing him into the addition. She put her hands on her hips as he began to rummage through an open crate. "Can I help you find something?" Her voice trembled between laughter and frustration.

"A vase." He held up the rose. It wobbled on its stem. "Maybe some water will fix it up."

Tish found a test tube and stand. "The faucets don't work inside. Maybe they haven't been connected yet."

Outside, Tish left footprints in the dusty trail to the creek that in high summer was merely a thin silver trickle. She waited patiently for enough water to me-ander down the creekbed to fill the test tube, and by the time she walked back to the barn, Mitch had spread a pristine white linen cloth in the shade of the eucalyp-tus grove for which the creek had been named.

Smiling at his forethought, Tish set the drooping bud in the test tube and placed it exactly in the center of the tablecloth. His romantic impulses seemed to come in brown paper bags. He folded the one that had held the cloth and emptied another to reveal a crock of pâté, a crusty loaf of sourdough bread and...a bottle of wine.

Surprised and touched, Tish abandoned thoughts of the full picnic basket in her car without hesitation. "This looks marvelous," she said. "You really do mean to do it up right, don't you?"

He handed her a glass of cut crystal. "Yes." His voice was terse.

She looked down and bit her lip. "Mitch? There's a price tag stuck inside this glass."

He frowned. "Did I miss one? I only bought this stuff this morning."

"For now? To—to make an occasion for me?"

"Of course, for you. I don't keep tablecloths and junk at home." He swore softly.

"What's the matter?"

Mitch looked disgusted. "I've never had one of these before, either." He held up one of the fancier versions of corkscrew. "How do these things work, anyway?"

"You need a degree in wine making to know that. Here, I'll do it." She gently took the gadget from him. "Were you going to have anything to drink?"

He looked startled that she'd ask. "I brought some mineral water from the springs in Calistoga."

Smiling, Tish put the corkscrew and bottle back in the paper bag. "That's what I'll have, too, if you don't mind sharing."

"You know I don't mind sharing with you, but is there something wrong with the wine? What do you call it? An inferior vintage?"

"You must know that it's an extremely superior one," she said sternly, pulling the top off the pâté container. "That label had to have cost you a fortune."

Mitch grinned like a boy caught doing mischief. "I went into the wine shop and asked for the best they had."

"They certainly sold you the most expensive. You don't have to impress me by spending your money. It's enough that you wanted to go to all this trouble for *me*." She said the last word carefully, with the uncertain emphasis of a child who isn't quite sure the treat is for her, after all.

"It wasn't any trouble. I like doing things for you." The frown came back as he studied her. "The wine's yours because, well, because I wanted to show you we have a chance. Even if there are differences between us. We can handle anything together."

"Can we? Oh, Mitch, maybe we can!" She threw herself into his arms enthusiastically and knocked him backward. Laughing and panting, they kissed with an openmouthed ferocity that became tender, and then ceased altogether when Tish lifted her lips gently from his so she could watch her finger trace the curve of his ear.

He pushed them both upright. "Drink your wine. No back talk."

"I don't need any wine. The only aphrodisiac I need when I'm with you, is you."

His shirt was fastened with fancy little mother-of-pearl snaps, not buttons. They offered a definite temptation to a woman set on seduction. Instead of ripping them all open in one grand sweep, though, Tish took her time, slipping her thumb inside his shirtfront and flicking open each separate snap with a deliberation that racked her nerves—and, she hoped, his.

His voice was hoarse. "Letizia, you'd better be damned good and sure that what you're going after is what you want. Nobody's going to come bumbling out here to your rescue."

The last snap unsnapped. Slowly and luxuriously, Tish pulled the shirttails out from the waistband of his jeans. She pushed the shirt open and saw the shoulder holster, with its grim black contents. Her fingers trembled as she forced the fabric off his big shoulders. They continued to shake, just a little, as she unbuckled the holster straps that wound through the narrow arc of chest hair.

"What makes you think I want to be rescued?" she asked bravely.

Mitch let her fumble with the strap, although he could have had it off and discarded in one second flat. A determined scowl had replaced her siren smile the moment her tormentingly slow movements had revealed the gun. This was her real gift to him, just as his had been the wine—gestures so outrageously out of character they couldn't be misunderstood. *This is for you. We can handle anything together. This is for you....*

He ran his hands through her hair, liking the way individual strands clung to his fingers. Sunlight struck blue highlights in the thick black waves. She had worn it down today, lovemaking-style, and he bent his head to bury his face in it.

Finally the stubborn strap gave way. He straightened so she could pull the holster off over his head and lay it aside. Tish had to rise up on her knees to do it; turning back toward him, she accidentally brushed her breasts against his cheek, and then he ruthlessly stole the initiative away from her.

He gave her the same treatment she'd given him, except that he paired the uncoupling of each button with a kiss of the warm skin his fingers revealed. Then he reached the satin and wire of her bra. No mere scrap of silk could have sufficed for a woman with her pleasing abundance; Mitch felt his loins turn to water, then fire, as the sun danced over the shadow between her breasts. There was something unbearably erotic about so much firm, creamy flesh waiting for his touch, waiting to be unveiled to his sight—his sight alone. Following an impulse he wouldn't have had with any other woman, he paused to look into her eyes.

"You're so beautiful," he said hoarsely.

Her lids fluttered and he saw her swallow. "Why are you stopping?" she whispered.

"I guess—to let you know you're important to me. *This* is important, not just . . ."

She opened her eyes. "I'm glad. I couldn't bear to be just a temporary sexual convenience to you. I want—" She bit her lip.

The sight enticed Mitch to lean over and bite her lip, too, very lightly. Gasping, she found his hands and placed them on her breasts. Against his mouth, she begged, "Don't stop. Oh, Mitch, this time, please don't stop."

He dealt with her blouse with more speed than finesse, then brought her against his chest, into his arms. Her sob of desperation was accompanied by a frantic scrabbling of her fingers at the zipper of his jeans. A ragged sound escaped his own throat as his tongue lashed the soft pink tips of her breasts. Her shorts and panties came off in a tangle of cotton and lace.

Sitting up was too much trouble, Tish realized. Her breasts throbbed with pleasure. One of his fingers was stroking deep inside her. She moaned at the dizzying sensation. "I get drunk on you, Mitch. I lose myself in you. How can that happen?"

"I don't know," he answered, groaning as she pushed away his jeans and briefs to close her palm around his erection. "You do it to me, too."

Somehow he found the condom; in moments they were joined. They gave up all attempts at control.

They rolled. He lay atop her, plunging deeply. Then, so quickly she barely had time to savor the feel of him, he pulled her over him in one deft movement. Sighing, she straddled him, leaning forward and back, discovering the positions that gave her the most pleasure. Her wild ride began urgently and ended with a climax of pleasure so hot and piercingly sweet that Tish collapsed against his chest, hugging his hips tightly against hers to encourage the quick, hard thrusts that brought him to satisfaction.

Their movements gradually stilled. Tish listened as Mitch's heart continued to pound under her ear.

Raising her head after long minutes, she kissed him softly and wriggled slightly to free herself. His hands, which had been stroking her bare, perspiration-damp back, moved down to curve gently over her buttocks. "Stay," he said.

"But—aren't you . . . Are you comfortable?"

"Oh, you honey. I'm very comfortable. I seem to be getting more comfortable every minute." He moved suggestively to prove it.

Tish was amazed at the ripple of desire that radiated out from the penis, sheathed and potent inside her. "I didn't know men could . . . recover this quickly."

"Neither did I," he admitted blithely. "It's never happened to me before. You probably shouldn't count on this every time, but right now you seem to be doing things for my stamina." He moved again, and he watched her face and her tangled hair and the increasingly rhythmical undulations of her body.

Her gaze met and held his, her intent expression changing to the glaze of desire and excitement. Reluctantly, Mitch withdrew to replace protection and then pulled her astride him once more. Her voice low, she said tentatively. "We could switch places. I'd like to feel how—how heavy you are and how we'd fit together."

Mitch scooped up some pâté on his finger and brought it to her lips. He smiled as her tongue swirled up the tasty spread with delicate precision. He shushed her with his finger against her lips and spoke gently. "No, ma'am. Not out here. You stay right where you are. The ground's too hard and you bruise too easily."

Tish watched him looking at the mark on her neck. She kissed his finger and put her hand over his, moving it to where she knew the bruise stood out in gaudy purple and blue. She said, "I can't even feel it."

"Can you feel this?"

The fingertip meandered in a sensual trail down her flat tummy to her damp black curls. His hand slid between their bodies. His hips surged upward. Doubly stimulated, she arched backward as ecstasy threatened to explode inside her. She couldn't, she daren't say I love you, although she knew that only love, and Mitch, could account for such mounting, aching, burning pleasure.... As her eyelids drifted shut, her gaze fell on the half-opened crock of pâté next to the gun, snug in its holster and tangled in its straps.

Civilization living with brutality. The familiar mocked by the terrifying.

Then his fingers moved again and she forgot everything but Mitch.

12

FEELING LANGUID AND SORE and remarkably happy, Tish pulled on her shorts and top. By concentrating on buckling her sandals, she carefully missed the sight of Mitch donning his holster. When she spotted denim out of the corner of her eye, she lifted her head to watch him resnap all his fascinating mother-of-pearl buttons.

"That's a terrific shirt. I'll bet it was designed by a woman with a fabulous imagination."

His smile was lazy and pure male. "Liked it, huh? Come to think of it, I'd enjoy seeing it on you. And especially seeing it come *off* you."

Laughing, she evaded his arms and picked up the earthenware crock. "You can't be in that mood again!" She sniffed the pâté dubiously.

"My mood's perfect. Unfortunately, the rest of me needs to recuperate for a while. You deserve a lot of loving, and I'm not eighteen anymore." He grinned, patently unconcerned about his age or virility.

"Excuse me, Sheriff, sir," she shot back at him, "but I'm pretty sure you didn't hear me complain about the quantity or the quality of the loving. As far as that goes, would you want to be a teenager again? I wouldn't."

Some of the carefree grin faded, and Tish cursed herself for reminding him of the horror of his early life. "Can't say that I'd want that, either," he said quietly.

"I think this has been in the sun too long." She held up the pâté, hoping to distract him.

Some of the tension left his shoulders. "Sorry to hear that. I worked up an appetite."

"I'm starting to learn about your appetites," she answered sternly. "There's the bread and—actually, I brought a few things to picnic on, too. The basket's in the car. I'll get it."

A packet of ice gel she'd tucked in among the plastic containers had kept the food cool. Munching on a curried chicken wing while Mitch attacked the potato salad, she led the way back into the barn to retrieve her notes and purse.

In the dim interior the wooden barrels looked huge, large enough to drown a couple of men standing upright, and the carvings that decorated them took on a nightmare quality. The sculpted faces seemed to grow gargoyle noses and chins that wavered in the uncertain light.

"This place gives me the creeps," Mitch said from the doorway.

"What? Mitch, it's an ideal building!"

"If you say so."

Mitch heard the cold, flat note in his voice. Tish seemed to withdraw from him without moving an inch. His fault, he knew, and he tried to make himself stop.

"Forget it. Without the electricity on, the room has a certain chamber-of-horrors effect, that's all."

A minute ago, with her lips pink and swollen and her hair mussed, she'd looked happy and sated. Thoroughly loved. Now the full mouth curved down. All the spring went out of her stance as her spine straightened and her shoulders squared. "Chamber of horrors? Because it's being made into a winery?"

"Yes," he replied truthfully, hating himself.

"So much for 'We can handle anything together.' In case you were wondering, I haven't decided yet if I'm going to get involved in Eucalyptus Creek," said Tish. Only after the words were out did she realize that she'd again echoed Mitch's phrase for whatever it was they had begun together. *I'm involved with you, all right,* she thought with a spurt of joy and desolation. *How long can we be happy?*

He made an impatient gesture and looked surprised that he still held the tub of potato salad. He put it down on a box of pipettes. "Let's not pretend with each other, okay? You're dying to throw in with your family on this little enterprise. You light up like a Christmas tree every time the subject comes up."

"I'm starting to get just a little fed up with the way people around here assume they know what I've decided before I do!" she shouted, astonishing herself. "Just cut it the hell out, will you?"

You-you-you echoed among the rafters. Tish's eyes widened until they almost lost their almond shape. "Oh my God, Mitch, I yelled at you."

"I noticed." His mouth softened. "Honey, what is it? You're white as a sheet."

"I yelled at you," she repeated in a tiny voice.

His shaggy brows drew together. "So, what's the big deal? We're lovers, dammit. You know me. I'm not going to shoot you for standing up for yourself."

A visible shudder ran through her. "No. No, of course you wouldn't."

There was something wrong here—severely wrong—but Mitch didn't know what it was. Trying to defuse the situation, he said, "I'm sorry I brought up the whole subject. It's your money and your life, and you're the only one who can figure out how to manage them."

He reached out and pulled her to him. His lips traced her hairline, and his tongue tasted the salt of perspiration caused by their lovemaking. He felt comforted by the reminder of their elemental joining a brief half hour before. She meant something to him, over and above the remarkable sex, and he liked the tangible evidence that he meant something to her, too. "Let's just get out of here, okay? It really does give me the creeps."

"Okay." She sounded normal again, but she pivoted in his embrace so she was tucked under his right, holsterless, arm. As they ambled toward the exit, she said, "You know, drinking doesn't have to be abusive. My whole life, I've never seen anybody at one of my family's parties under the influence. Most drinkers aren't problem drinkers. There's a theory that a gene can be inherited, which creates a chemical imbalance and predisposes some people toward abuse. But having it doesn't automatically make a person an alcoholic, and not having it doesn't mean he—or she—won't become one. As long as you remember moderation in all things—"

Mitch didn't want to talk about wine anymore, so he grinned. "*All* things?"

Tish shook her tousled hair at him, locking the door firmly. "You're fishing for a compliment."

"Well, I wouldn't object if you happened to have one handy."

She kissed him warmly. "You make me feel a lot of things," she whispered with a husky catch in her voice. "And none of them is lukewarm." Remembering the definitely immoderate passion that had blazed between them roused more damp heat within her. She leaned into his strength and lifted her hips to rub against his.

He wrapped his arms around her. It was hot outside, desert hot, but now she reveled in the sunshine.

"You're no bigger than a minute through here," he murmured, sliding his hands down to clasp her buttocks.

"You and Nonna. You both want me to grow into some fat Italian mama."

Mama just slipped out. The word implied babies, and Tish hid her face in his shoulder so Mitch couldn't interpret her expression. She felt the rumble of his laughter. "Honey, I'm not stupid enough to complain about perfection."

"I ought to get back," she said reluctantly. "Everybody's no doubt on tenterhooks waiting to see the results of the latest bombshell Pa dropped on me."

Mitch draped a possessive arm around her neck, steering her toward her car. It was his left arm. Despite a determined effort, she didn't seem to be able to relax against the hard, unnatural bulge of his holster.

Her stiff avoidance of the weapon clued Mitch in. *Not stupid, huh?* he jeered at himself. Feelings, his old enemies, jostled in his gut. Uncomplicated sex with a casual partner had never resulted in this internal emotional battle. He was falling for her—falling hard; wanting all the real, sane, sweet things that made life worth more than the compulsive routine he'd used to hold himself together since Carol had died. Mitch didn't have any idea in hell if he could handle falling in love.

Falling in love with a woman who obviously hated what he did for a living. She hadn't repeated a single one of the love words she'd poured onto his wounded spirit the other night. None. There'd been a flood of them then, and an absence of them today. He had a vague conviction, based on experience, that women making love liked to whisper or moan or scream endearments. His previous bed partners had all tossed endearments into intimate conversation, whether the relationship had been serious or not. As a sort of sexual courtesy. Certainly he didn't want Tish to manufacture meaningless bedroom chatter, but no *sweetheart*, not even a halfhearted *dear*?

Casually, he moved his arm from her shoulders. Sometimes the best way to get at the truth was to surprise it out of someone with a change of topic. But this wasn't just someone, it was his Letizia. Squashing down guilt firmly, he remarked, "I'm taking a friend to a civic dinner next Friday. I have to go—I'm speaking. The date was set up a while ago. I'd feel bad about breaking it...."

"I can't exactly complain," Tish said, wrinkling her nose. "There aren't two civic dinners that night, are there? I have a date for it myself."

He'd been caught in his own trap, Mitch realized. Male instincts flaring, he spun her around. "Who?"

Tish went absolutely still in his grip. "Mitch, don't."

Too late, he remembered that her ex-husband had been the jealous type. Cursing, he let her go. "Sorry. I scared you again, didn't I?"

"A little." Her smile was a poor effort. "Not your fault. I mean, a normal woman would be flattered that you . . . cared. The date's with Tommy DeCarlo. I only said I'd go out with him because—" She looked down, then up at him. "Because you never called."

Sudden mischief danced in the depths of her dark eyes, and some of the guilt and outraged possessiveness that had a stranglehold on his throat eased. "My mistake, obviously. I was—oh, damn, I was scared if we spent any more time together we'd start something I wasn't sure I could finish."

Tish didn't want to talk about the inevitable finish between them. Cautiously she returned to the previous subject. "I'd cancel Tommy but it's awfully short notice. It really wouldn't be fair." Mischief flickered again. "And this way I can check out your taste in dates. It wouldn't be someone who likes blue sequins, would it?"

His *mmphh* suggested that it probably was. Unlike Tish, petite Suzie could no doubt wear a flashy, form-fitting gown. Despite the young woman's declaration that her boss wasn't a big enough fish for her matrimonial net, Tish couldn't dismiss a slight churning in her stomach at the thought of Mitch squiring anyone so damnably cute.

She pulled his hand to her cheek. She tried to believe he was regretting having asked Suzie, or whomever. "Okay," he said, "you can drive to the dinner with Tommy. You can leave with Tommy, but by God you won't go home with him. Got it?"

Her chin lifted. "On the understanding that the same applies to Blue Sequins."

"A deal." His slow grin alleviated some of Tish's unease.

They packed up the picnic gear. As Mitch tossed containers into the basket, Tish lifted the rose from its makeshift vase. The bud still dangled forlornly. "I guess this didn't make it."

He plucked it from her hand. "Don't look so sad. It's not an omen, Tish."

She watched as he laid it carefully in the exact center of the square of crushed grass where the tablecloth had rested. A smile touched her lips. Her hard-edged cop had some very romantic facets indeed. "Of course it's not an omen," she agreed, but they avoided looking at each other.

He tucked her into her car, giving it a glance of disbelief. "What happened to the heap?"

"One of Pa's buddies fixes up cars. He did everything out of the goodness of his heart. Like a fairy godfather. My family and their friends really are wonderful. I'd like to live closer to them but, Lord, they're pushy."

Full sunlight bathed Mitch's narrow face, and Tish told herself she was imagining the shadow creeping across it. "Yeah. Love is like that."

"Does it have to be?" she asked, thinking of guns and jealous, domineering men.

"I don't know." For the first time that day, the old expressionlessness had returned, as if he wanted to shut her out. "I only know it hurts to picture you with another man."

Tish tried to be honest without being reckless. "I don't want to be with anyone except you."

She looked back as she drove away. Mitch was staring balefully at the stone barn, future home of Eucalyptus Creek Winery.

"WE DIDN'T EXPECT YOU to be angry so long, Letizia."

Pa's hangdog look was well practiced, but Tish still fell for it. "I'm not angry—much. I'm concerned. How long have you had that mortgage hanging over your heads?"

"Four—no, five months. It is a fifteen-year note, so we save on interest over a—"

"Stop trying to bamboozle me. You never got all that work done out there in a lousy five months. Contractors take that long just to pick up a hammer."

"You act as if we had no friends." Pa sounded huffy for a moment. Then he waved his arms expansively and reeled off several names she recognized. "We are old acquaintances of the builder, the plumber." He winked. "Even the building inspector. Magda has organized her share of teas for political candidates, too, over the years. Thank God for it. The zoning ordinances have become unbelievable."

Tish was horrified. "Just how many laws did you get around?"

Pa laughed. "We would never break the law, Letizia. You know that. We only got it to work a little faster than usual. You'll have no worries to distract you when you start getting Eucalyptus Creek off the ground."

She put her hands to her upswept hair, relieved. "We've been over this before, Pa. I haven't decided about Eucalyptus Creek yet. And I'd appreciate it if you'd—"

"Stop fussing with your hair. It is perfect. You are perfect."

Tish let her hands fall. "Thanks, even if you are trying to distract me from saying I haven't made up my mind about you-know-what."

They smiled at each other. Tish wouldn't claim to look perfect, but she was pleased with her appearance. Her black silk crepe evening dress had off-the-shoulder sleeves, and the chemise style hinted at the richly curved body underneath. On a shopping expedition with Belle, she'd found some pretty and obviously faux earrings to match its rhinestone buttons. Not much sparkle to compete with blue sequins, Tish reflected, but she hoped it would be enough.

"Tommy DeCarlo won't be able to keep his eyes off you," Pa told her.

It wasn't Tommy she wanted to attract.

The doorbell rang. Tommy ushered her into his ostentatious new German car. Tish nodded and made appropriate comments as he told her things she already knew about tax-free municipal bonds. The heavy odor of his cologne was overpowering.

"How do you open the window?" she asked, defeated by the array of buttons on the door beside her.

Tommy patted her hand. She had to make a conscious effort not to withdraw it. It wasn't his fault he wasn't Mitch. "No need. I'll turn up the air-conditioning." He pushed a button.

Tish fought back a sneeze in the torrent of frigid air. She pressed into the luxurious upholstery for warmth. And got set to endure the ride to Santa Rosa.

They arrived fashionably late. Tommy stopped to introduce her to half the people in the room, it seemed, so the main course was already being served by the time they reached their table. Her annoyance at the proprietorial grip he'd kept on her bare shoulder in the face of the other men's assessing glances increased when she was seated near a pillar. It was impossible for her to catch a glimpse of Mitch or his date.

Tish did her best to ignore her disappointment. She followed the animated discussion of real estate during the prime-rib dinner. Tommy's enthusiastic endorsement of strip development made her grit her teeth in order to keep her own opinions to herself. Then, in self-defense, she retreated behind the facade she'd perfected during her marriage, widening her eyes to simulate interest and murmuring appropriate inanities whenever the conversation flagged.

At last someone tapped a spoon against a glass. Mitch walked from one end of the head table to the podium and microphone at its center.

Mitch wore a dark gray suit, light gray shirt and a bolo tie. In contrast, Tommy's European-cut jacket looked a little too slim, too tailored. Its obviously expensive tailoring and accompanying promise of security no longer impressed her.

Mitch's speech was short and sweet. She agreed with his message about community efforts to keep crime out of rural areas. The audio system exaggerated the slight, excitingly harsh edge in his voice. Halfway through the talk, he loosened the string tie, unbuttoned the top button of his shirt and leaned confidentially over the podium as his eyes swept the room. When they met hers, they stopped.

He kept her still and rapt under his gaze throughout the rest of the speech. Once he'd finished, he left the microphone and accepted slaps on the back and hearty handshakes from the others at the head table, and in a very short time he'd cut a path through the crowd to her side.

Right behind him, sequins dazzled under the overhead lights. "Hello there! Nice to see you. Wasn't Mitch's speech great?"

It took a moment for Tish to register that Suzie's enthusiastic comments were really intended for Tommy.

"Does everybody know everybody else?" Mitch made the introductions, and then with a smooth movement Suzie inserted herself between Tish and Tommy.

"No, I've never met Mr. DeCarlo, but of course I've heard of him. So many people say such terrific things about that new mall you're . . . Well, if you want me to call you Tommy, you'll have to call me Suzie. . . ."

Mitch tugged his tie a little looser and grinned down at Tish. "Dance?"

"We shouldn't. I'm not here with you, remember?"

"I remember." His mouth went stern. "You should be, though."

"Yes, Sheriff," she answered meekly. "Maybe next time you'll ask me instead of someone else. In the meantime—"

"Tish? Is it okay for me to call you Tish? I'm going to ask Tommy to dance. Do you mind?"

Tish suppressed a giggle until Tommy and Suzie were safely out of earshot. "She's a fast worker, isn't she?" she asked, catching the glitter of blue sequins now and then in the swirl of bodies moving to a blare of the swing band's sax.

"DeCarlo didn't look like he objected. Dance with me."

"Oh, Mitch, if we do I—I won't want to stop at dancing."

His voice almost lured her into his arms. "Would that be so bad?" he asked.

"Out in public in front of your constituents?" She managed a light, shaky laugh. "I can see the headlines now—Local Sheriff Arrested For Lascivious Conduct."

"We don't have to spend the whole night in public. In private we can be as lascivious as we want. Have you been thinking of me? That way?"

"*Yes,*" she said, pushing his hands away. "Behave yourself. I've got a date, and I'm very sorry but I'm not the kind of woman who shows up with one man and leaves with another."

Mitch surrendered and led her to a seat in a dark corner. He pulled her hand to rest on the gray herringbone covering his thigh. Her wrist jerked in automatic reaction to the sexual tingle that arced between them, and his grip tightened.

"Are you going to punish me all night for bringing Suzie?"

"Of course not." Tish tried to stop her fingers from stroking the light wool. He needed to lighten up, she decided. "I was betting on the dress. I must say, you must be a dream to work for. I've never heard of a boss who picks up his secretary's dry cleaning."

To her surprise, dark color ran from his jaw to his angular cheekbones. "I bought her the dress, Letizia. She didn't have anything to wear and she joked about it, but she really wanted to come to this dinner. It was in payment for a lot of favors."

"You're a fraud, you know that, Sheriff?" she said softly. "You pretend to be so rough and tough, and inside you're a complete marshmallow." Jealousy flared. "What kind of favors?"

He laughed. "Platonic ones. Guarding me from cop groupies at affairs like this."

"Ladies who get turned on by handcuffs," she muttered under her breath. "Why I have so much faith in you..."

"Sweetheart, if you can't trust the law, who can you trust?" he asked aggrievedly, and she laughed. But fear stirred. Mitch could bend her to his will with a joke and a smile. And whether or not he currently had anything going with Suzie, the detestably cute blonde must be used to law enforcement and was therefore a better match for a career cop. She shivered.

His arm swept around her shoulders. "Cold? Have I told you how much I like what you're wearing?" he murmured in her ear.

His warmth pushed away the fears. "Not yet." She smiled. "Go ahead."

He did, dwelling on how much more he'd like it when she wasn't wearing anything at all. Tish let her head rest against his sleeve and enjoyed the faint, clean smell of his after-shave. If he carried a gun, she couldn't detect it.

She was vaguely aware that the band had swung from one old hit to another. Neither Tommy nor Suzie reappeared. However, a young waitress intruded. "Champagne, ma'am? Sir?"

Mitch ignored Tish's feeble attempt to free herself and kept her cuddled close. "Honey? Would you like some champagne?"

She murmured no, and the waitress left. "Really, Mitch, the last thing I need around you is a drink. You and wine form a pretty lethal combination."

"What's that supposed to mean?"

His sharpness puzzled her. She pulled back. "Why, just that — Oh, I might as well admit it. At Nonna and Pa's reception when you kissed me, I didn't feel quite as sober as I thought I should. I kept telling myself it was the Zinfandel, but in fact it didn't affect me until the moment you—" A slow, delighted grin played around his mouth. She looked down her nose. "Don't look so smug. So your kiss intoxicates me. It's probably just some form of temporary insanity." *Perhaps not so temporary,* she thought, and brushed the notion away.

"Yeah." His grin went crooked and he looked at the mass of gyrating dancers. "I drove down to the city last week, the day before we—had our picnic. I meant to visit my mother. We haven't talked in, I don't know, ten years."

"Ten *years?*" gasped Tish.

"One of her neighbors keeps track of her for me. He calls or writes if she needs anything or the garbage piles up too high on the sidewalk. You know, I couldn't make myself knock on her door. I just stood there for a while and then I got back in the car and drove around for hours."

"Mitch." Real shock muted her voice, but whether it was at a son's avoiding his mother for such a long time or a mother who merited such treatment, she wasn't sure.

"I guess I'm too sensitive about remarks about alcohol. With my mother the way she is... Well, you said it yourself. The problem can be inherited."

"Is that what you're afraid of?" she asked bluntly.

He shrugged. "I tried the stuff once. My insides were in knots, while I wondered if I'd do some sort of Jekyll and Hyde. Anyway, the drink didn't do whatever it's supposed to do as far as I could tell. I mean, I didn't feel relaxed and happy or even woozy. Just sick to my stomach and uptight as hell. It didn't even taste good. Sorry," he added, lifting a finger to her cheek. "I know that's heresy."

Turning her head, she pursed her lips against the finger. "Not especially. I don't expect you to like everything I like. Believe it or not, once a month at, er, a certain time, I get this absolute craving for chocolate—"

"That's not so unusual," said Mitch.

"And jalapeño peppers. Not chocolate-*covered* peppers, mind you, but chocolate and peppers during the same meal."

"So we'll find a Mexican restaurant with spicy food and you can order a mousse for dessert," he suggested tenderly.

Tommy waltzed by with Suzie in his arms. He didn't appear to be missing her, Tish decided. Despite the fact their dimly lit corner didn't really offer much concealment, she put her arms around Mitch's neck. "Can we go to your house now and make love all night?"

Mitch looked into Tish's slightly flushed face and half-closed eyes and felt his heart begin to pulse with heavy, sledgehammer strokes. "I think that can be arranged."

"Because a man who understands about chocolate and chili peppers deserves all the attention he can handle. And I intend to keep you *extremely* busy."

13

THE FOUR OF THEM gathered briefly to collect wraps. Suzie cuddled close to Tommy and gave Tish a surreptitious thumbs-up. She and Tommy didn't seem to think the change of escorts required comment, so Tish simply studied an industrial-grade framed print on the wall until Mitch took her hand in his and led her out of the hotel.

The doorman sent a valet to locate Mitch's car. As Tish stepped off the well-lit curb, a sudden thrust from the side sent her stumbling against Mitch. She grabbed at him to keep from falling. A sharp tug on her arm made her cry out. The gilt buckle on her evening bag's strap dug into the soft flesh near her elbow. The strap held and the would-be thief raced away into the darkness on his ten-speed. It was over in an instant. The tension slowly drained from Mitch's body. He swore. "Are you all right? Get a look at him?"

"Yes. No. You didn't pull your gun."

He drew her back onto the curb, into the dead black-and-white illumination of the streetlamps. "Couldn't." His tone was rich with self-disgust. "I left it in my car. Not that I would have endangered citizens by shooting at some two-bit bicycle thief—probably a kid, anyhow. But I feel sort of naked." He moved his shoulders uneasily.

The incident had passed so quickly, no one else seemed to be aware of it. Tish bit her lip. "The valet's brought your car."

The trip to his town house was accomplished in silence.

A question repeated incessantly in Tish's mind. *Why wasn't Mitch wearing his gun?* Finally she ventured, "I guess I thought you always carried a gun of some sort."

"Usually I do."

"But not tonight."

"Tonight I knew I'd be seeing you."

There didn't seem to be any answer to that. She felt joy mixed with pain. When would he begin to hate her for getting between him and the tools of his job?

They were driving down dark but well-frequented roads. The headlights of an oncoming car sent a wash of silver over Mitch's features, and the image of his profile lodged in Tish's mind like a still photograph. Then another car sped by, and as if by magic the picture became completely different. The lights caught Mitch glancing at her, frowning in concern, as if he were pondering a question.

"You okay? We don't have to go to my place. I can take you to Gus and Magda's, instead."

Tish sat up straight, very carefully folding her hands. "If you don't want me in your home . . ."

"Honey, you know that's not true. It's just that— Hell's bells, woman, I'm trying to say I'd understand if you didn't find getting mugged a form of foreplay. You're entitled to a good cry or a monumental snit or just wanting to be alone."

"I'd rather be with you," she said quietly.

He sighed. "I hoped you'd say that."

About the time he pulled into a garage, her body started to shake with delayed reaction and he wrapped his jacket warmly around her before leading the way to his condominium. Flicking on the light inside, he slammed the door with his foot. Then she was in his arms, clinging shamelessly.

"I'd like to think this was passion," he said after a few minutes.

She drew a deep, steadying breath. "I'm acting like a fruitcake. It's so dumb. He didn't even get my purse and here I am, quivering like a leaf."

"You're not used to being a victim." His jacket fell to the floor. Mitch moved his palm in comforting circles on her back.

The soft, hunted look in her brown eyes intensified for an instant. Then her lashes swept down, creating fascinating little fans over her cheekbones and she whispered, "Are you going to make love to me?"

He released some of his steely control and pulled her hips tight against his. A murmur escaped her throat. Since he'd caught sight of her sitting next to Tommy but staring at him, his wayward imagination had been conjuring up provocative memories of what was hidden under that discreetly tantalizing dress. He found the zipper with his fingers and pulled it down slowly, erotically, to draw out the aching pleasure of the moment and to give his Letizia time to shift from one kind of need to another.

She wouldn't let him give her any time, though. An impatient wriggle dropped the dress to the floor in a puddle of silk. She would have rid herself of the black strapless bra and tap pants just as quickly but Mitch muttered, "Let me." She reached for his shirt, unbuttoning it so frantically one of the buttons popped off. Her urgency fed his own desire and he picked her up and carried her to the rug in front of his fireplace.

Kneeling over her, he said thickly, "To answer your question, no, I'm not going to make love to you. We're going to make love to each other."

"YOU'RE TICKLISH!"

"Not—not ticklish, exactly."

He trailed one rough fingertip over her abdomen and watched in delight as she undulated under his light touch. "I like finding out what gives you pleasure."

"I can see that." Her eyes widened at the visible resurgence of his erection and then fluttered as he followed his finger with his lips and moved lower. The firelight flickered, casting a red glow over two perspiration-slick bodies. The only sound competing with the crackle of the fire was her panting. At last she wailed her pleasure aloud, and he moved over her, filling her before the shattering tremors ceased.

"I want to be the only man you ever hold like this."

She enfolded him with arms, legs, and the tiniest, most secret muscles of her body.

His voice roughened. "Call me something special—as if you—loved me."

"Oh, babe. Love. My love."

He kept on whispering, demanding, causing gentle ripples of sensation to spread through her again…and again . . . until his own release shook him.

MITCH REBUILT THE FIRE, and Tish propped her chin on her hands.

"What did this rug start its life as?" she asked idly.

He poked at the logs one last time and sat back on his haunches, smiling appreciatively at her long limbs and rosy skin. Tish snuggled into the pelt before the tiled hearth. "A bighorn sheep."

She swallowed a yawn. "Poor sheep."

"You're right, but in my grandfather's time, bagging a trophy head or pelt wasn't an environmental issue. I vaguely remember him holding me on his lap, telling me about his hunting and fishing trips into the Rockies. A great big guy, a U.S. marshal. The kind of guy you could trust to stick with you to hell and back."

She smiled. "Like his grandson."

"Thanks. I'd like to think so. I've heard my father was like that, too, but he died when I was one." Tish unsuccessfully tried to suppress another lazy yawn.

"Tired?" Mitch asked, smoothing a wayward curl behind her ear.

"A little. Tell me more about your granddad."

Mitch hesitated, his hand still in her hair. Then he got to his feet and reached above the oak mantelpiece. Tish rolled over so that she could admire the clean lines of his back, legs and buttocks.

He turned. "This was his rifle. In fact, it's the one that killed the ram." Holding it out to her, he said coaxingly, "See the stock? Hand carved, like Gus's vats. You don't see work like this anymore. It's not loaded, Tish. Even the firing mechanism is gone. It's ornamental. There's nothing to be afraid of. You can touch it."

"Mitch, I don't want to touch it. Everything's been so perfect, don't let's spoil it—"

"For me. For us. You were able to handle my shoulder holster."

"The holster, not the gun." Gracefully she moved into a cross-legged position, but he saw her tension in the rigid pose of her head and arms.

For her own good, he thought. Her reactions to firearms were extreme. "Don't think of it as a gun. Look at it as a statue of a gun," he urged.

Even in the firelight, her face paled. "What is this, some kind of psychological conditioning? Get the little girl with the phobia to touch what scares her so she'll get nice and desensitized?"

Her defensiveness failed to hide her terror. Mitch spoke carefully. "I thought maybe you could appreciate it for its antique value, if nothing else."

"You were wrong. Amateur night at the psychoanalyst's is over!"

She scrambled up. The hope Mitch had cherished that she'd overcome her fear of firearms crumbled. Backing into the entryway, she snatched up her clothes and awkwardly hauled on her underthings.

"Letizia, for God's sake! Look, I'm putting the damned thing back. There, it's on the wall. It can't hurt you. Don't stare at me like that, honey. Please. It breaks my heart."

Her sobbing breath sounded shockingly loud against the gentle crackling of the fire. "I'm sorry, I'm sorry, I'm sorry, but I can't help it. You looked like a savage. Naked in the firelight with a weapon in your hands. Face it, I'm not going to get over how I feel about guns and—and people who use them."

"The rifle's not any more dangerous than a big stick—"

"Not just that gun. *Any* gun! My ex-husband collected them. Hundreds of them. He was in the gun room the day I told him I was leaving him. He—he—"

Mitch quickly crossed the room, taking the dress she was mangling in her attempt to pull it on, and smoothing it over her hips and zipping it up for her. "Did he shoot?" he asked, trying to keep his voice normal.

"Three times," Tish got out.

"God."

"He was trying to scare me out of asking the court for my share of the community property. He shot over my head and then when I ran, at my feet. The third shot went through the door after I made it out. I was so afraid and so mad. I shook all the way to the lawyer's office. But I was determined that he wasn't going to scare me out of a decent settlement. It wasn't the money, although I wanted it to put into a winery. It was the principle. If I hadn't fought back, I wouldn't have been able to respect myself for the rest of my life."

"I'm proud of you. That took a lot of courage." Mitch felt a fierce surge of respect for her.

Her smile was little more than a grimace. "Well, I was proud of me, too. There wasn't very much of *me* left by that time in my marriage. I had to—to rebuild myself into a real person. It was hard. I won't let myself be scared into being somebody's plastic doll again."

"You think I treat you that way? Or think of you that way?"

"No. I can tell you're not like him. Maybe I don't know how to trust a lover. I look at your guns and handcuffs and speed loaders and I know you'd never turn them against me. But the man I was married to promised to love me and protect me, and he picked up a gun and pointed it an inch from my face and pulled the trigger. I can't forget, Mitch. I've tried, I've really tried...."

"It's okay to be scared. Listen, all this stuff can go in a closet. You'll never have to look at it again."

He was holding her very gently, and he felt her shoulders, her whole body sag. "But that's not fair, either! You shouldn't have to give up things that mean something to you. That was your grandfather's rifle, for pity's sake. It's beautiful, even if it scares me to death. And the rest of the equipment is gear you need for your own defense. To protect other people."

"No, I don't, Tish. I'm a desk jockey these days, honey. My most valuable weapon is the telephone. It's about time I admitted it and stopped riding ramrod over drunk drivers in my free time."

She looked at him wonderingly. "You'd do that for me?"

Strong emotions tore at him. "Yes. Marry me, Letizia. I don't know if we can make it work but—marry me."

Tish moaned as if she were in pain. It hit him, hard, that this was his woman and he was hurting her by asking her to marry him. What if there was something wrong with him? What if she could tell it was impossible for him to hack it as a husband? He'd always been a loner, and he'd certainly failed the first time around. . . .

"Oh, God, it's tempting," she replied, assuaging his fears. "But, Mitch, we wouldn't have a chance. You're talking about having to hide your possessions in your own home. And it's part of your job to ride with your deputies. You told me so yourself. Don't bother to give me any garbage about how you'd shirk your duty."

The tension in his gut eased, too. "You wouldn't let me, would you? We can do it. We can make a marriage work."

"Oh, Mitch. I'd never ask you to compromise your work. But what if I can't control my feelings and it gets to the point where you have to choose between our marriage and your job? I'm terrified my fears would make you less than you are. You're a special breed. You shouldn't have to change because I'm, well, gun-shy." She smiled ruefully at her own pun. "Besides, remember how you feel about what I do for a living."

"You don't have to connect up with Eucalyptus Creek if you don't want to," Mitch said quickly, and then damned himself. He'd already sworn he wouldn't attempt to influence her decision.

"Sure," she jeered. "Tell me my grandparents who raised me haven't sunk hundreds of thousands of dollars into this project. Tell me I'm not uniquely qualified to lead it. Tell me it won't kill them if I walk away."

Linking his hands behind her neck, he sighed and leaned his forehead against hers. "And you want to throw in with them."

"Yes. It's about time I admitted it." Her chin tilted and her lips brushed his mouth, but Mitch could sense her desperation as she jerked away. "What are we going to do?"

Mitch actually felt twinges of pain as he unclenched his fingers one by one and stepped back from her soft warmth. He was suddenly and angrily aware of his nakedness. "I'm going to get dressed."

Tish leaned heavily against the wall as he padded down the short hallway and into another room. She was right; she knew she was. Unless one or both of them changed fundamentally, a marriage between them would be an unqualified disaster.

Being right wasn't much consolation for being miserable.

The ride to the D'Angeli house was quiet and nerve-racking. Mitch was waiting to say something more; she could feel it in the way he glanced at her from time to time, moistening his lips and opening his mouth, then closing it again. Finally, as he pulled up inside the circle of light from the porch bulb, he grated out, "I'm not willing to stop seeing you."

Tish let her finger trace one of the rectangles that patterned his sweater. By chance—by design?—she rubbed the nipple beneath the thin wool so it stood out in shallow male arousal, silent testimony to the attraction between them. The possibility that she'd never see Mitch again made her heart lurch painfully.

"Mitch, we're just so different—"

"No. We're the same. Both of us have had lousy experiences with other people."

She shrugged helplessly. "Granted. But you know all the reasons why we're wrong for each other. Even if we tiptoe politely around our prejudices, we'll end up hating each other, and ourselves, in the end. You can't stand wine and I panic over guns. Maybe I'm too selfish to risk any more pain for either of us."

"Letizia, you're the most loving, giving person I've ever met," Mitch said, cupping her chin. "I have no intention of letting you loose on the dating scene for some other man to snap up. Now you'd better get inside. It'll be dawn in two hours. Dream of me," he ordered.

Tish knew she'd dream of him, all right, but she murmured stubbornly, "On one condition. Don't try to get in touch with me this weekend."

"In a pig's eye."

Quickly, to keep him from dissuading her, she said, "I have to go back to Cupertino on Wednesday. I can't let the cork-sniffing department down by jumping ship without notice. Belle's giving a Fourth of July barbecue on Tuesday. Think things over. Maybe the short-term benefits of being together aren't worth the long-term grief. That's all I can promise, Mitch. Short-term. If you can't live with that . . . Well, we can talk about it at the barbecue."

Naturally Mitch chose the one piece of information that she'd hoped he'd miss in her rush of words. "Then you're definitely buying into Eucalyptus Creek."

"Yes." She looked out the car window at the roses, their velvety black heads nodding in the darkness. "Yes."

He drummed his knuckles on the steering wheel. "I'm not crazy about putting a time limit on an emotional commitment. An affair? Honey, you're just not that kind of woman."

"Short-term is the way it has to be."

As if she hadn't said it, he walked her to the door with his arm around her shoulders to protect her from the cool night air. The hard bulge of his holster, strapped again across his chest, was impossible to miss, but Tish didn't comment on it. She couldn't blame him for putting it on again—not after the attempted purse-snatching. There wasn't anything left to say, she thought despairingly.

Mitch waited until she'd opened the door, then said curtly, "Lock up behind you."

Too late, she almost said aloud. *You've already captured my heart.*

As quietly as she could, Tish undressed and washed off her makeup. She got into bed and lay unmoving until the rising sun tinted the morning fog a pearly pink. She missed Mitch. Stern on the outside, sensitive on the inside. A wonderful lover—considerate and demanding by exciting turns. The kind of man who happened along once in a woman's lifetime—if the woman got very, very lucky.

The man she'd just sent away, perhaps forever.

Restless, she rose not long after dawn. Slipping outside in jeans and a windbreaker, she wandered through the vineyard, occasionally breaking a grape off to taste. She'd always loved the long rows of vines in the early morning mist.

The kitchen light blazed behind gauzy curtains. Tish answered its mute invitation, softly closing the door behind her.

"You're up early." Nonna stopped placing silverware in precise patterns on the table. "Or have you not been to sleep? You look wretched."

Tish tried to smile. "I'll come in on Eucalyptus Creek."

"Letizia—"

"Something has to be understood, though. My money goes in, too. And we're finding some nice safe place for some of your money that the bankruptcy courts can't touch. In case I blow it and the winery goes bust, I want you and Pa to have some security. That's not negotiable, so don't argue." She paused, but Nonna only tilted her head consideringly. Tish added, "Don't you have anything to say?"

"Why?" asked Nonna. "You're an adult business-woman. We trust your judgment. And we can always use the money later for the winery if it becomes nec-essary. But it won't."

Tish explained it all over again to Pa when he came down to breakfast, along with her ideas for developing a premium line of varietal wines. He stopped her sev-eral times to dance her around the table to the violin strains of Nonna's radio music. Laughing, Tish fell into step with him, and tried not to think of last night when she hadn't danced with Mitch.

14

ROW HOUSES PERCHED staircase-fashion along the slope of one of San Francisco's steep hills. The neighborhood had an air of age, neglect and decay. The buildings seemed to lean against each other for support.

Mitch retrieved a key from under a flowerpot that held a plant's brittle skeleton. A miniature living Christmas tree, maybe—the kind sold in grocery stores? He stopped for a moment to study the sad little twig. How many years had he spent without any tree— or Christmas spirit—at all?

Temptation beckoned. He didn't have to go in. He could walk way. Again. And face a lifetime of holidays alone, without family and without Tish because he couldn't make peace with the specters of his past.

Bracing himself, he turned the key and stepped inside. The woman who looked up from the sofa was, he knew, just middle-aged. Harsh light from the window struck her, deepening every hollow and crag of a thin face that had once resembled his own. Today she could have been a hundred years old.

"Mitchell?" Her mouth fell open. "Mitchell, baby?"

"Mom." A wave of pity swamped any anger he felt. He bent and placed an awkward peck on her cheek. "How many times have I told you it's not safe to leave your key under a flowerpot?"

"IF YOU DUST THAT mantel one more time," Belle drawled, "you're going to take off the finish."

"I suppose," Tish murmured absently, lifting a photograph of her father. She rubbed the dustcloth gently and thoroughly over the ornate silver frame. "Know what I think?"

"What?"

"That since my parents died I've spent my whole life searching for security in the wrong places. Look at Jonathan."

"Ick. Do I have to?"

"He seemed so full of self-confidence, while really he was hollow inside. Money certainly doesn't buy happiness. It would be nice if it did, because cash is much easier to come by than wisdom, but it doesn't. Take it from me."

Belle lounged in Pa's recliner and regarded her cousin with amusement. "Okay. What brought on all this heavy-duty philosophizing?"

Letting it all out in a rush, Tish blurted what she'd told Mitch. "I think I must be crazy," she finished miserably.

"I think you must be, too," Belle said with calm tactlessness. "Give the guy some room, cuz. A sheriff has to carry a gun. Sometimes they're darned comforting things to have around."

"True." Mitch had pulled his weapon to protect her from nonexistent burglars, and hadn't carried it to prevent her from becoming upset even before he discovered the reason for her anxiety. He'd never tried to dominate her. "I can't seem to convince myself I don't have to stay battle ready, waiting for him to pull a big macho act."

Belle snorted. "You got burned once and you're scared. Everybody has old memories that get in the way once in a while. Grow up, Tish."

"Mitch has had some unlucky experiences to deal with, too. He's dead set against Eucalyptus Creek. He looked at that beautiful job the builders have done at the stone barn and said it was a chamber of horrors."

"So, both of you need to grow up."

Tish replaced the photograph. "We'd better do it fast. I told him we'd talk some more at your barbecue but not to expect more than—than—"

"Sleeping together."

"An affair." Her hands fell to her sides. "What if he doesn't show up?"

The kitchen timer shrilled and they rushed to pull blackberry pies, juice bubbling through golden crust, from Nonna's oven. "Six," Tish counted, placing them beside previously baked desserts. "Will that be enough?"

"With the ice cream the kids'll crank fresh, it ought to be. Of course," Belle added, with a sideways glance, "it depends on how much Mitch eats if he's at the barbecue."

Tish refused to take the bait. "You've still got that ancient ice-cream maker? I would've thought you'd have replaced it years ago."

"Are you kidding? The new ones are electric. No effort at all. How would I keep my hellions from spending the Fourth blowing themselves up with fireworks if they weren't cranking?"

Belle would be a font of tips about child-rearing, Tish thought, if she and Mitch began a family.... And then the whole horrible, crushing load of fears and hates seemed to break over her in an overwhelming wave. It was unlikely that they'd have any future together, let alone one that included children.

Just the unbearable tension of waiting for their love to die would kill that future.

If Mitch loved her. He'd made masterful love to her, asked her to marry him, but never said the words. Wiping up a pool of spilled blackberry juice from the counter, Tish wondered if, as far as Mitch was concerned, they were still just "involved."

"When will the grands get back from church?" Belle asked, interrupting her thoughts.

"Not till late. They were going out to the coast."

Belle frowned. "I hope Nonna drives if it's after dark. Pa's night vision is getting pretty undependable."

Night vision. Tish didn't even have to close her eyes to see Mitch, his lean angles half-lit in the fire's flickering glow, as he settled his weight lightly over her. She could almost feel Mitch above her, the ram's pelt below....

"A guy down the road from my house has an apartment he's getting ready to rent. He'd let us look before he advertises. You want to take a peek?" At Tish's blank stare, Belle continued impatiently, "I'm assuming you don't want to live with Nonna and Pa permanently."

"Good Lord, no! They've been perfect darlings, but—"

"Uh-huh. We'll take your car and you can show me how that sexy new sunroof works."

The apartment was over a carriage house. It had a large freshly painted bedroom, a modernized kitchen and a miniature, perfect marble fireplace that Tish fell for on sight. With dark wicker furniture and lots of flowers . . . "Can I let you know on Wednesday?" Silly to wait until then; whether Mitch made an appearance at the barbecue or not, she'd need living quarters of her own. She'd been the one to specify a short-term affair. It had been her decision not to marry. Still, instinct wouldn't let her make final plans.

THE NEXT DAY, Tish walked into the bank.

"Tish! Tish, over here!" She recognized Suzie's uninhibited shriek. Tommy and Suzie were waving to her.

Suzie dragged a chair from a nearby desk and sat beside Tish in the New Accounts executive's cubicle. A spanking new diamond glittered like hoarfrost on the secretary's ring finger.

"He proposed at four twenty-three Saturday morning," Suzie bubbled. "I won't tell you exactly what we were doing at the time—"

"Jeez, Sue." Tommy sounded pleased rather than embarrassed.

A crazy sense of relief flooded Tish. Thank goodness, she'd never be asked to date the handsome and oh-so-boring real-estate agent again. And Suzie, so much more suitable a mate for Mitch than Tish, would be busy picking out a trousseau to match that oversize rock on her left hand.

"This is a real whirlwind romance," Tish said, smiling.

"Hey, there's the guy I have to see," Tommy interjected. "I'll be right back."

Suzie's snub features softened as she gazed after him. "He's fantastic, isn't he? I didn't believe there were any cute rich heterosexuals around anymore."

Despite Suzie's glowing face, Tish had to ask, "Do you love him? Oh, I know it's not any of my business and this'll sound like a corny country-and-western song, but it's true. Money won't make up for missing out on love."

"That's the unbelievable part! I do love him! I think." She made a comic face. "How do you tell if it's real or just the old biological clock chiming three-quarters to menopause or some kind of fantasy thing? You know, the prince roaring up in his BMW convertible to rescue Cinderella from her drab office job."

"You must be twenty years from menopause."

"Thanks, but I mean it. How do you tell the feeling's real?"

Tish's smile wavered. "When it hurts. And you still wouldn't trade it for anything."

15

"SIT DOWN."

The probationary officer shifted from one foot to the other and clasped her hands behind her back. Her wide leather belt was so new it creaked at every nervous movement she made.

"Sit!" Mitch said more firmly.

She sat. The young woman's professionally impassive face couldn't mask the anxiety in her eyes. She reminded him of Tish trying to deny that what they had between them was enough to build a life together. Doing his best to force Tish from his thoughts, and not succeeding very well, he summoned a friendly smile.

"It's rotten to get called in here on a holiday, I know. My secretary got carried away scheduling my time when I told her I'd had enough vacation. I'm afraid you're suffering for my bureaucratic sins."

He segued neatly into a speech he'd recited so often he almost didn't have to listen to himself. The honor of serving the citizens of the county, the duty to protect innocent and guilty alike when rights were being violated, the importance of maintaining an open mind toward the unknown, were all part of the job.

The unknown. Until he'd met the D'Angelis, nothing could have been less familiar to him than their kind of healthy, hearty home life. No doubt about it, the events of that life were well lubricated with vino. He couldn't recall one party thrown by the D'Angelis that had failed to include wine or beer.

Nor, he realized with sudden clarity, could he think of a celebration at which a D'Angeli or a guest had been the worse for drinking. He'd trust any of them to drive away from a party. Except Tish, of course. But her driving was in a class by itself that had zip to do with alcohol. So maybe his own reactions weren't so much a reasoned hatred of a chemical as a ten-year-old's desperate attempt to control a universe without rules.

Sunday, Mitch had taken his first stumbling steps toward patching things up with his mother. Perhaps they would learn to laugh and cry together. Some day. Who was he to give lectures on maintaining an open mind? From the start, his had been closed against his mom, her disease, and Tish's career.

Yesterday, he'd escorted his mother to a treatment center. She'd held her head up high as she walked to the desk where she'd signed herself in. The motto on a computer poster above their heads read One Day At A Time. That was the way lives were lived, after all. One precious day at a time. And he wanted to spend all his days with Letizia.

"Sheriff?" The recruit cleared her throat. "Was there anything else?"

Damn, had he drifted off in midsentence? Mitch didn't know and didn't care. "Can't think of a thing. Just do your best, back up your partner and—take it one day at a time."

Glancing down at his watch, he swore and bolted, leaving the young woman goggle-eyed as he sprinted through the connecting office to the elevators.

Suzie peered in. "Rats, I was going to tell him about a big old traffic jam on 101. You know, Fourth of July and all."

"Our boss is nuts," said the deputy.

"Naw." Suzie breathed on her diamond and rubbed it against her chest, holding it up to admire the sparkle. "He's in love."

"THIS REALLY IS GOD'S country," pronounced Belle's husband, surveying his portion of it from the redwood deck attached to his twenties-style bungalow.

Tish took the glass of iced tea Frank had brought her and added, "If you leave out the earthquakes and the fog and the mosquitoes."

Frank opened his mouth to argue the point but Belle cut him off. "Never mind, sugar. Tish is out-of-sorts because she threw down the old gauntlet in front of her boyfriend and he hasn't picked it up."

"I did not!" Tish defended herself. "It wasn't that way at all!"

"No? What do you call it when you tell somebody, 'Do it my my way or nothing?'"

Tish took a long breath. The deck was crowded; the backyard swarmed with children—some running back and forth through the smoke from the barbecue grill, others sitting among the branches of the Burbank plum. All in all, Tish's vantage point gave an unimpeded view of the party. Mitch simply wasn't there.

"What do I call it? Rank stupidity, I guess. 'Scuse me."

Weaving her way through the obstacle course of shorts-clad cousins, Tish heard Frank's plaintive, "Nobody ever tells me anything. Does Tish have a boyfriend?"

"I don't think even Tish knows the answer to that one," Belle replied.

Several guests stopped Tish to offer good wishes for the Eucalyptus Creek Winery or to say how happy they were that she was moving back to Sonoma County. She managed innocuous replies, making a wide circuit around Aunt Aurelia, who seemed intent on continuing her earlier lecture about aging divorcees who whistled away eligible bachelors. At last, she reached Nonna's chair, which was drawn up under the shade of a lawn umbrella. Nonna crooked a finger. "Letizia, Mr. Fontana is thirsty. Could you . . ."

"No, please," the old man said. "Don't bother."

Tish smiled. "How could it be a bother? You won't let me do anything to repay you for the miracle you worked on my car."

"I do not see it today. Is it running well for you?"

"Oh, yes," she hastened to reassure him. "But it seemed silly to bring two cars when Nonna and Pa were coming anyway. Now, what can I get you? A soda?"

He winced. "The carbonation gives me—" He fluttered an eloquent hand near his digestive tract.

"Oh, dear," Tish commiserated. "Iced tea?"

"Caffeine. My doctor has forbidden me."

"Remind me never to go to your doctor," Nonna put in.

"I'll check if there's some fruit juice," offered Tish.

"Don't. I haven't regressed so far into second child-hood." He sighed. "My gout has acted up or I would have some of that nice vino Frank is serving, but the medication can't be taken with alcohol. Ah, well. I see Gus. Excuse me, ladies."

"Where is Mitch?" Nonna demanded.

"Since it's after six, I presume he's not coming." Tish sank down onto the grass. Resting her arms on her knees, she hid her face. The darkness felt good against her closed eyes. It helped push back the tears. "I let him see how much I dislike his guns and things. And he doesn't love me enough to accept what I want to do with my life or to understand how I was raised. It could be he doesn't love me at all."

Nonna was silent so long that Tish raised her head and added, "There's something about me that either scares men away or makes them want to put me in my place. I thought I'd outgrown it or Mitch was different or something. He's not, though. It's just taken him longer to decide I'm not what he wants."

"I had at least hoped you'd learned to value your-self," Nonna said with more force than usual. Then her tone softened to its usual dulcet murmur. "You've been warmer lately, more open about how you feel. That does attract people."

Tish laughed without mirth. "Let's say I must be too much of a good thing. Anyway, he's not here, is he? Belle's right. It's my own fault. I shouldn't have in-sisted that he show up willing to see everything my way. God knows, I don't like being ordered around."

"An ultimatum? To a man like Mitch?" the older woman said disbelievingly. "Letizia, has no one ever told you the ultimatum is a strategy of war, not love?"

"Several people, now that you mention it. Oh, Nonna, I love him so much. I don't want to lose him— but it looks like I already have. I'd even try putting up with his macho sheriff stuff—"

Nonna's sweet voice could have cut steel. "How big of you. How generous. To tolerate his job. For your information, missy, a man deserves wholehearted support from his mate!"

"A woman does, too!" Grief filled her. "We've both tried, we have, but it's no use. He was smart to stay away."

"And you're glad, I suppose."

But even pride couldn't force Tish to whisper an agreement. Two lonely tears ran down her cheeks.

BOOM. SCREECH. "Aahhh."

The explosion of stars from the final bottle rocket in Frank's arsenal dwindled to a red-and-gold mist, then went out altogether.

Tish watched at the gray afterimage for a moment before it, too, disappeared. She felt just like it. Mitch was gone, and all the heat and color and brightness that he'd brought to her life had been snuffed out.

Sometime during the long twilight, she'd passed from misery to a blessed state of numbness. When Pa took the driver's seat at the end of the party, a dim sense of self-preservation prodded her to ask, "Uh, is Pa supposed to—"

"Shh," Nonna replied. "You will hurt Gus's feelings."

SWEATING, PUSHING AWAY an increasingly frantic sense of *too late, too late, too late,* Mitch leaped the low fence into Belle and Frank D'Angeli's yard. It was brightly lit; the bigger boys stared at him in admiration.

"Where's your Aunt Letizia?"

"Who's— Oh, it's you, Mitch." Belle came out onto the deck. "She left with the grands about forty-five minutes ago."

"Which route?"

She raised her brows in exaggerated semicircles at his terseness. "Old Redwood Highway, I'd imagine."

He remembered to shout, "Thanks!" over his shoulder as he took the fence running again. The nagging premonition wouldn't leave him. He turned on the ignition and shifted with one hand, buckling himself in with the other, and sped into the quiet street, flipping on his lights and siren once more. *Too late . . .*

SEATED IN THE REAR behind Nonna, Tish could see the way Pa hunched over the wheel, poking his head forward like a turtle and continually blinking his eyes as if to clear them. Her concern for her grandparents' safety grew. She edged toward the middle of the back seat to use Nonna as a barometer for how well Pa was driving. He was following the car ahead rather closely, Tish thought. Nonna was in a better position to see than Tish. She appeared serene and relaxed—too relaxed, Tish realized. A ladylike snore sounded.

"Pa? Oh, my God, look out!"

Taillights seemed to climb over the hood, then vanished in a crunch of metal and a tinkle of glass. In hideous slow motion, Tish lurched forward in her seat belt. It held, and jerked her back against the seat. Her head bounced, finally slamming back against the headrest with a force that brought flashes of light to her eyes.

Scrambling from the car, bruised but in one piece, she wrenched open Nonna's door. Parts of old prayers spilled from her lips. Her grandmother stood unaided and said strongly, "I'm fine—see to Gus."

Blood from a cut on his forehead darkened one side of Pa's round face. He grunted, "My fault. Sorry. How is Magda?" So Tish knew he was all right, too.

Still, he was too shaken to do more than sit while she struggled to undo his safety belt. When a man's husky form loomed out of the darkness, she gasped thankfully, "Please, can you help me?"

The form weaved but Tish couldn't spare him more than a quick glance. "Whassa matter with ya? Y'all blind? Ya ran righ' inna me. I oughta—"

A heavy, sour whiskey smell washed over Tish. She gave the clip mechanism a desperate yank, freeing Pa as the other driver mumbled, "Bran' new pickup. Lookit what ya done. I know what I oughta do. I'll get even...."

Then Tish saw him clearly. He held something in his hands and he was swinging it. She screamed silently, *Mitch!*

HE SAW THE ACCIDENT before any of its victims noticed him coming. All the participants were in motion as he pulled up, and only stopped in their tracks at the sudden silence when he cut the siren. In the glare of his headlights, the elder D'Angelis had moved together, holding each other up, as Tish stepped between them and a hulking guy who gripped a tire iron.

A sort of autopilot clicked on in a primitive part of Mitch's brain. *I'll take him out if he touches Letizia. I'll by God take him out.* He walked in an easy, unthreatening rhythm until the man swiveled to face him.

Well over .10 blood alcohol and stupid with it, Mitch noted. *Not falling down, though, and mean drunk enough to be dangerous. Standing entirely too close to Tish and her grandparents.*

Mitch dismissed the idea of using the gun tidily holstered under his suit jacket. Now that he was too far from his radio to use it, he realized he'd forgotten the first lesson a cop learns. Never walk into a situation without calling for backup. His fear for Tish and her family had driven his training right out of his head. Smiling carefully, he reached for his wallet and flashed his badge, although he doubted his quarry could focus enough to identify the symbol. "Sheriff's Department. Had some trouble here?"

"See wha' they didda my pickup. Teash 'em a lesshon—"

"Looks to me like they've already learned the lesson," Mitch said soothingly. "Their insurance will pay for the damage, make your pickup good as new."

The last word set the drunk off again; although the tire iron had dipped toward the ground, now it lifted again, to waver near Tish's head. "Bran' new pickup—"

Struggling to maintain an even tone, Mitch drew on all his years of practical psychology. It felt like a small triumph when his monotone coaxing brought forth the information that his adversary answered to the name Rafe. But with the infuriating persistence of the very drunk, Rafe stayed between Mitch and the D'Angelis, covering them with his blunt weapon, until Mitch's palms grew wet and his fingers itched for physical action. His gentle Letizia, too, he saw, tensed every time Rafe's blurred gaze shifted slightly. A red tide of fear blinded him as he recognized that she was ready to jump Rafe at the first opportunity.

She'd get her skull bashed in.

The realization cleared his vision. His decision made, he let his hand begin it's inch-by-inch journey to his holster.

Abruptly Rafe dropped the tire iron. The burly man sat on the ground, legs outstretched, purple face crumpled in a baby's yowl. "My beau'ful pickup. I like i' bedder'n my wife. I like i' beder'n havin' *sex* wif my wife. . . ."

Snorting with disgust, Mitch eased the iron out of Rafe's reach and read him his rights. Then he said, "Honey, bring me the cuffs from my car and then use the radio to— No," he corrected himself at the sight of her white face and shaking hands. "You've never handled the radio, have you? Use my car phone. Call 911 and get us some backup. Go!"

Tish ran, cursing her rubbery knees. The handcuffs hung from the turn signal, as always. She brought them over to Mitch. He cuffed Rafe and with an official frown he turned to Nonna and Pa. "All right, who was driving? Rear-enders are usually chalked up as the second car's fault, but I'm willing to concede Rafe might have made himself pretty hard to miss."

The tiny silence that followed was long enough for Tish to compute the long list of loving favors her grandparents had done for her, and the irreparable damage to Pa's pride if he lost his driver's license. Mitch's opinion of her skill behind the wheel was minimal at best. She could tell a lie, or half of one. Not even the unattractive Rafe, who was muttering to himself in a maudlin singsong, deserved the blame for an accident he hadn't caused. "It wasn't his—that man's—fault. And I was driving."

How odd, she thought. Here she'd just taken the responsibility for causing a crash that might result in a nasty fine or the temporary loss of her own license.... And now that shock was wearing off, joy poured through her in tangible waves. Mitch had come after her. There was no other reason for him to be on this particular road. She smiled brilliantly.

Pa's stunned intake of breath brought her partway back to earth. "Letizia, it is twenty years and more since I spanked you. I never believed I would be tempted to do so again."

"Pa—" she said warningly.

"No more pretending," Nonna directed. She exchanged a rueful look with Pa. "Forgive me, Gus, but I for one would be relieved if you didn't drive anymore."

Pa added, "Mitch, this bambina needs a talking-to. I was the driver. My old man's foolishness wouldn't let me admit my eyes—they aren't so good at night anymore. It is all my fault." He hung his head, his bald spot a pale reflection of the rising moon.

Mitch said only, "Tish, I need that backup. Don't worry, Gus, Tish and I are going to have a long talk in the near future. You'd better give me your license now."

Chastened, Pa obeyed. After making the call, Tish rejoined the group with a wary eye on the man she loved. He might consider that he had more than one legitimate nit to pick with her. He stood very tall and formidable in the glow of moonlight and headlights.

Majestically Nonna said, "A talk can cover more than one topic of interest. In fact, whole discussions have been held without any words at all. I recommend it to both of you. And, Letizia, don't feel sorry about Gus. He has better ways to prove his virility than by driving a car."

Delivered in Nonna's best grande-dame manner, the remark killed the conversation. However, Tish could see Pa's expression brightening as Nonna wiped the blood away with a handkerchief. Even Mitch was having trouble keeping his expression serious, Tish noted. He caught her looking at him and pulled her into the shadows. "A good, long talk," he growled in her ear. His smothered laughter spoiled the hint of threat.

"If that's what you want." Her whisper was rich with the promise of seduction.

"Right now I don't know if I want to strangle you or make love to you standing up, so don't push me, lady."

"You won't strangle me," she said with newfound confidence. "Or beat me or shoot me with your great big gun."

"Don't be so sure. Maybe you aren't aware of it, but 'gun' has—uh—a sort of special connotation. I mean, it can refer to a part of a man's body when it's in a certain condition. Like it's getting now when you rub up against— Hell, honey, Gus and Magda are fifteen feet away!"

"And very carefully looking in the other direction. Besides, I told you, they lust to grandparent your babies." She held her breath, waiting for his reaction.

"I doubt they want to watch one being conceived in a ditch at the side of the road," he said, holding her tightly for a moment before he firmly set her aside. "Let me guard that crazy drunk, will you, so he doesn't try to kill any of us again?"

"Rafe's gone to sleep," she told him. A dozen pieces of information jostled at the tip of her tongue and the hell of it was, Mitch was right. This was a perfectly lousy place and time to try to make him understand all the things that suddenly seemed so crystal clear.

Patrol cars began to zoom in. The sight of uniforms sobered a roughly wakened Rafe as Mitch's badge had not. With unexpected coherence, he said, "I didn't mean no harm. Shouldn'ta had so many drinks, but you understand how it is. The guys, they expect you to order a man's drink, not some sissy soda. . . ."

A deputy deposited him in a squad car and drove him away. Under Mitch's vigilant eyes, others measured skid marks while one inspected Nonna and Pa's car. Tish shuddered at the accordion pleats in the hood. Mr. Fontana would have his work cut out for him.

A freshening breeze from the ocean kept the goose bumps riffling up and down her uncovered arms and legs. Finding a stump out of everyone's way, she sat huddled with her arms around her legs, Rafe's pitiful excuse for getting drunk pushing other, more immediate matters from her mind. Mixed up in there somewhere was the comforting image of Mitch's freckled hands. They were gripping the neck of a bottle of wine. But when had Mitch ever . . . ?

A new crop of gooseflesh rose all over her. The cause wasn't cold. It was excitement.

"Letizia? Letizia!"

She looked up in a daze and blinked. The deputy was handing Pa's key ring to Nonna and saying, "Pulls a little to the left. As long as you compensate for that, you'll be able to drive fine. Miracle your headlights are still functional."

"It's a night for miracles," Nonna said softly. "Hadn't you noticed?"

Joining Pa, who was sitting on the passenger side, Nonna stuck her lovely white head out the window. "We'll see you—when we see you. Mitch, I know we can trust Letizia with you." Her eyes twinkled merrily. "And, my darling granddaughter, we can trust Mitch with *you*."

She drove Pa away. Mitch darted a significant glance at the deputy, who grinned and said, "I'll make sure they get home safe and sound, sir, ma'am," and followed them in his car.

That left one patrol car, plus the sheriff's own vehicle. Tish touched the back of her head and flinched, feeling muddled.

Mitch noticed—he always noticed, she thought—
and he said, "We should have a medic check you over.
Are you dizzy? Sleepy? Count my fingers."

She looked into his face, not at his hand. "Ten."

"Oh, God. It was three. Harrington, call an ambu-
lance. No, wait, I'll run her to the emergency room
myself. Come on, honey. Here, I'll carry you."

"This is very nice," she said as he swept her into his
arms and started toward his car. It was, too. The hard
muscles of his arms and chest cradled her tenderly. That
was Mitch, she thought, little though he would have
liked the description; power sheathed in gentleness,
sensitivity merging with strength. "Really, though,
there's nothing wrong with me. Just a harmless little
bump on my head."

"So we'll have a doctor look at it and tell me it's
harmless."

Another snippet of information slid smoothly into
place in the riot of new speculations going through her
brain. She buried her face in his shoulder to hide a grin.
Imperiously she said, "I want to go in the squad car. Put
me in back, please."

She couldn't see but could sense the exchange of
glances between Mitch and the deputy over her head.
"Women," it said as plainly as a shout.

"I'll want to lie down and the patrol car is wider," she
added.

Mitch shifted one arm so he could cover one of her
ears and simultaneously pressed the other ear against
his chest. She caught only muffled spurts of the ensu-

ing discussion. "Concussion . . . Not usually unreasonable . . . Humor her. . . ."

She'd get Mitch for that last crack, she decided, although given what she planned to do, it might be just as well if he convinced himself she was suffering from a brain injury. A trickle of fear over his reaction weakened her determination. Perhaps she should consider the score even already.

He freed her ears, still holding her cradle-fashion in a strong embrace. "Harrington, you hold the door while I slip her in." Harrington seemed to respond well to orders. "There, Tish, are you comfortable?" Mitch asked, leaning into the car so he could arrange her in a semireclining position on the wide back seat.

"Oh, Mitch, you're always so good to me," she murmured and then quickly, before she could lose her precarious nerve, she twisted her head, looked down and gasped, "Mitch, look!"

He acted instantly, as she'd known he would, propelling himself forward to protect her from whatever it was that had put the urgent note in her voice. As his legs followed him fully into the car, Tish shouted, "Harrington, shut the door!"

Her tone of command worked. The door slammed shut.

16

"THE BACK SEAT of a police car doesn't have inside handles," Tish pointed out after a moment of stunned silence. Mitch lay half across her lap, the expression on his face not unreadable at all.

His string of curses ended with, "That means we're locked in!"

Tish judged it safer not to reply. She caught his hand before he could knock on the window to signal Harrington to let them out. "Wait, please. I'm not concussed and I'm not crazy." Well, she was, but only about one very big and mad-as-hell sheriff. Hurriedly she continued, "If you drag me off to a hospital we'll be there for hours with forms and tests and they'll stick me in one of those tacky paper nighties and—that's not how I want to spend the rest of the night with you."

"You'd rather be here?" He sounded incredulous.

Her fingers walked up his chest to loosen the turquoise clip that held his bolo tie. "Are you saying you've never had one teensy wicked fantasy about something you'd like to do with a woman in the back of a patrol car?"

"How'd I get trapped in here with a certifiable sex fiend?" he wondered aloud.

"I did it," she admitted, then cocked her head as his words sank in. "You are trapped, aren't you?"

"*We're* trapped, lady. You and me. I hope you're not claustrophobic. The mesh shield is up between us and the front seat, these doors won't work from the inside and the windows are sealed. We'll be in here till that idiot Harrington lets us out."

"Don't you want to be alone with me?" Tish asked softly.

"There's a question designed by a woman to get a man in trouble if I ever heard one. Of course I want to be alone with you. I've just spent six lousy hours untangling the biggest monster traffic jam I've ever seen trying to get to you. However I think most objective observers would conclude that this isn't the best place for what people normally do when they're alone. I'm going to yell for Harrington."

"Wait! Not yet. I want to savor this. I've really got you trapped!"

"Yes, Tish." His voice held a note of warning. "And if you gloat about it, you may find out exactly what angry men do when they feel trapped. I can just about guarantee you won't like it."

Tish put a fingertip to the corner of his mouth where his teeth gleamed in a fox's predatory grin. She couldn't resist teasing. "I probably wouldn't. But you aren't going to—to constrain me against my will, or even pretend you'd force me just to get us all turned on—"

He had her flat on her back in two seconds. "I don't need that to enjoy sex with you."

"I know." She smiled sunnily. "You don't have to prove it, especially to me. You can let me up now."

"Oh. Sure." Glowering, Mitch made room for her to sit up. Instead, she leaned back on her elbows. He had to lean into the shadows of the seat to hear her low murmur.

"The point I was trying to make is that— Lord, I suppose this will sound strange. You didn't trap me, I trapped you. I was the hunter. It's really sweet of you to let yourself be caught like this."

"You're doing this because of the handcuffs, aren't you?" he asked resignedly. "I kidded you about them and you're never going to let me forget it. I'll be doomed forever to this weird sex life using law-enforcement equipment in kinky, degenerate ways. I'm terrified to imagine what you'll come up with for my speed loaders."

"I could hang them from—"

Mitch kissed her, fast and hard, to cut off her offer. His blood pressure was already within stroke range. Tish's eyes were meltingly soft with mischief and invitation, no longer clouded by the wrenching sadness he'd seen the night she'd sent him away. She did away with his tie and progressed to his shirt buttons. He knew the seductive game she was playing and discovered he felt absolutely no impulse to stop her.

When the door behind him inched open, he snarled without looking around, "What is it?"

"Er, Sheriff, you want I should let you out now?"

"Does it look like I want you to let us out, Harrington?" he demanded in exasperation.

"No, sir."

"Then close the door," Tish suggested in her melodious voice. "I have personal business to discuss with the sheriff."

"But, sir, what you want I should do while you and the lady—while you—while you take your personal time, sir?"

"I'm going to have to check this man's personnel file. You're supposed to have a measurable IQ to get into the department," Mitch muttered. Loudly, to cover Tish's giggles, he said, "Get in my car. Here're the keys. Drive. Drive for an hour. If you tell a soul where we are I'll keep you investigating violations of the leash law until retirement. Doggy-doo patrol. Got that?"

"Yessir!"

"And make a lot of noise when you get back. We might be busy."

"Yes *sir!*"

They lay unmoving until the sound of Mitch's car faded away. They sighed at the same time and smiled. Sitting up, Mitch pulled Tish into his arms and kissed her, this time long and deeply. "I'm going to make love to you," he muttered against her lips.

"You can count on me to cooperate, Sheriff." Her fingers trailed along the arrow of hair that pointed downward past his navel and then tormented him with light, suggestive touches as they released his belt, button and zipper.

Mitch captured her hands and held them between their bodies. "The back seat of a car is a ridiculous place for this. I'm six-three and you're damn near six-feet—"

"Five-eleven and three-quarters," she whispered, wriggling her thumbs free and drawing them slowly across the hollows of his palms. "Want to make something of it?"

"Only that we're not going to fit."

"That's odd. My recollection is that we fit quite nicely."

The smooth, rhythmic friction against his palms dragged a groan from him. "Yeah. Okay. Talk to me, though."

"What do you want to hear?" She varied barely whispered, sexy murmurings with quick, moist forays of her tongue into his ear.

"There's not a thing wrong with that.... Tish, honey, I went to the city. To visit my mother."

She pulled back and met his gaze. Mitch gave her a little smile, loving the glow of joy and silver moonlight on her features. "Really? Oh, I'm so glad. Did—did everything go all right?"

"There were some rough spots. We have a lot of history to overcome. The best part is she's gone into treatment. First time. She seems determined; I think she has a chance. I'd like you to meet her."

"I'd be honored." Tish touched his face tenderly. "When you showed up like the cavalry riding to the rescue, were you chasing after me?"

"Of course. Belle told me which way you'd gone. Letizia, I'm sorry I didn't make the barbecue. Sometimes even a siren can't clear the traffic around here. I got stuck on the freeway. Did you think I wasn't coming?"

Her nod was a mere shifting of shadows as she bent her head and raven-black hair rippled down to hide the pale gleam of her face. "I was afraid you didn't care enough to show."

He took a deep breath to cover the pain that stabbed him. With swift movements he began to straighten his clothes. "You couldn't trust me to get there if I could?"

"I trust you with my life," she said intensely. "You saved my life tonight. You didn't need a gun, but I trust you to know when one's necessary." She sat very still and looked at him soberly. "About the guns. I'll never much like having them around but I know they're safe in your hands. When Rafe was waving his tire iron, you know what I kept thinking? *Why doesn't Mitch just put a bullet into him?*"

"I'm not letting you within a mile of any of my weapons," Mitch told her sternly. "Next thing you'll be turning into a trigger-happy mama."

She shuddered. "I don't think so. But I do understand better why you carry them. Are you sure you want to be married to me, Mitch? I probably gave you second thoughts with all those stupid things I said about a short-term relationship. . . ."

"Believe me, lady, I've been shooting for 'forever' with you since the day after we met. I just couldn't admit it to myself."

"I love you," she whispered. He pulled her into a hard embrace.

The hum of insects penetrated the closed windows. Because she wanted to hear a particular gravelly note in his voice rather than out of a need for the words themselves, she asked, "You mean it's not enough just to be involved?"

"Our involvement is permanent and it's going to be legal as soon as possible. I love you, too, woman."

A fierce joy filled Tish, startling her with its intensity. The words must mean something, after all. The stuff that could form a family, that held a private universe together for man and woman.

"I think I like hearing 'I love you.'" She turned her head and kissed the inside of his wrist. "Would it bore you to say it again?"

He stroked her hair. "I love you. I love your warm heart and how you always make me feel like I've just come home. I love your sexy body and the gleam in your eye when you think up some depraved way to provoke me with it. I'll love all of you when we're both old and gray, and you'll be able to turn me on when I'm so old our grandchildren will think it's gross." His kiss was a long, lingering promise. "Hopefully by then you'll have had enough of fooling around in the back of police cars and we can have a king-size bed like decent senior citizens."

"With black satin sheets. A water bed, maybe."

"Water beds are all right. They slosh, but at least they stay warm. But satin sheets are slippery.

"How do you know all this stuff? Aha. Your misspent past is showing, Sheriff."

His wicked grin was fleeting. Tule fog began to gather in the hollows and bends of the country road. "Look on the bright side. I can save you miserable nights on cold, rumpled sheets."

"My nights with you have never been miserable—of course, we have yet to finish making love on any kind of sheets at all. Just think how adventurous a regular bed will seem."

"That's about as much adventure as my blood pressure will stand. Will it be enough for you?" She could feel the weight of his gaze in the darkness. "One bed. Mine. Kids underfoot. And if there are surprises along the way, they won't be the kind that end in divorce. No outs. Compromises, yeah, but not in how much we love each other."

She slid her arms around his neck. "Would you mind if we had the wedding at the little chapel in the field? Where Nonna and Pa got married? It would—feel right, somehow."

"Yeah. I'd like that."

Their mouths met, searching for intimate secrets as if it were the very first time. With aching gentleness his teeth nipped at the fullness of her upper lip. Her tongue peeked out, stroked his, circled his. Then he was above, holding her face in strong, safe hands, his tongue plunging into her mouth in lovemaking rhythm.

Between urgent kisses Tish finished ridding Mitch of his clothes with shameless efficiency. There was no place for innovation or thought in the flurry of mouths and limbs in the confined space. Shadowy glimpses of Mitch excited her. Passion-glazed eyes that were bright in the near darkness. His skin. A flat nipple. A sudden, tight grin. The outline of his erection, blunt and strong and unmistakably waiting to fill the hot emptiness aching inside her.

Her top and shorts and underthings ended up somewhere beneath their tangled arms and legs.

"Lovely Letizia— Hon, sorry, I forgot you don't like to be called that."

"I love my name when you say it. It's who I've become. Who I really am."

Letizia gulped for air. The sound of Mitch's breathing filled her ears as they struggled to maneuver long limbs in the cramped space. They were too aroused to laugh at their antics. All of Mitch's body fulfilled a fantasy for Tish; she pressed her lips, her tongue, against every part that came within reach of her seeking mouth.

"Some women really need handcuffs and all that law-enforcement stuff to get turned on?" she panted wonderingly.

"Uh-huh."

"All I need is one particular law-enforcement officer."

"Glad to hear it."

Her desire was hot and pulsing. His rough fingertips, so strangely gentle, so skillfully arousing, were readying her to receive him.

"Oh, Mitch, now."

"Take me home, Letizia. Call me sweet things. Say the words."

"I love you. Sweetheart. *Sweetheart.*"

Epilogue

"DÉJÀ-VU TIME," said Belle, hands on hips. She was swathed in dusty rose.

Behind her ivory veil, Letizia smiled. Her cousin's exuberance wasn't quite tamed to dignity, not even by the tailored suit and the stem of matching pink lilies.

"I saw Mitch a few minutes ago," Belle said. She swayed her hips. "I guess this outfit you and Nonna picked out is a hit. He said if you look half as good as me, the honeymoon's going to start in the limo on the way to the reception."

"He didn't!" Letizia clapped her hand to her mouth, and then hastily pulled the edge of the veil away from her lips to make sure pink lipstick hadn't smeared Nonna's fragile lace.

That eventful night, Harrington had dutifully returned in an hour to release her and Mitch from the patrol car, and to her knowledge he had never told a living soul about it. By that time, of course, the sheriff and his lady had been completely clothed and sitting a very proper half inch apart.

"Oh, well. I suppose it's about time Mitch stopped being so darned perfect and started blowing off a little steam," Letizia said philosophically.

In fact, he'd been so perfect he had taken over the million-and-one tiresome details necessary to turn two households into one while Letizia concentrated on Eucalyptus Creek Winery. And he'd lured her into going with him on his frequent visits to the foothills, where contractors were installing a bay window and marble fireplace in the house they would move into after the honeymoon. The place of honor above the mantel was reserved for his granddad's rifle. A very pretty, very private glade lay hidden from the rest of the world in the woods behind the house. Mitch always packed a picnic basket. . . .

In the moments between lovemaking, they'd planned the wedding. Organizing so many D'Angelis as well as Mitch's political acquaintances was a large task. Letizia had demanded, "How can you be so calm?"

"Easy. Families are fun. I never really had one before. Just don't try to put me in a dusty rose tuxedo."

"Oh? Is that a threat, Sheriff? What'll you do to me?"

He told her, in specific detail.

"Promises, promises." She'd laughed.

"You think I can't deliver? Don't forget, I know where you're ticklish."

"That's right," she'd said, winding her arms around his neck. "You do."

The sense of déjà vu strengthened as music swelled from the choir loft and the murmur of conversation in the very crowded chapel lessened. Mitch had put his foot down on the asthmatic organ, but a string quartet strummed the same march that had accompanied Nonna's walk up the aisle. Letizia gave a final twitch to the ivory gown her grandmother had worn two months before. Under the veil her black hair flowed past her shoulders, giving the straight, sumptuous lines of the twenties-style gown a medieval enchantment. The bridegroom's gift to the bride gleamed against the decorous expanse of ivory skin showing above the square neckline: A tiny pair of gold handcuffs on a whisper-thin gold chain wasn't really such an eccentric present for a law-enforcement officer to choose.

Her own gift to Mitch wasn't so much a thing as a promise. The demented number of hours she'd been putting in at the fledgling winery had paid off. As Mitch had slipped the chain with its charm around her neck the day before, Letizia had said, "What I have to give you isn't so romantic. It's a patent I've filed for."

"A patent. You've invented something?" He'd centered the charm at her throat and taken her into his arms.

"Uh-huh. The idea for it popped into my head the night we got engaged."

"When did you have time for that? Seemed to me you were busy experimenting with the practical limitations of the back seat of a police car."

"I didn't notice any limitations, Sheriff." He'd bent to kiss her then. His lips had coaxed her mouth open, her tongue had touched the tip of his, but she'd interrupted eagerly. "Listen a minute. I've been saving this up to tell you."

She'd explained the hot or cold filtration usually used to remove alcohol from fermented liquids, and how wine buffs claimed both processes left a beverage leached of flavor and the elusive, powerful magic called bouquet. "Then I thought, what if a winery—say, Eucalyptus Creek—started with a really superior vintage

and used a different technique altogether to get rid of
the dangerous chemical . . ."

"Spell it out, Letizia. Bottom line."

"The bottom line is that you've been right all along,
and I've been wrong. What I do for a living can de-
stroy lives. I'm ashamed I never faced it until that drunk
came at my grandparents and me with a tire iron. Eucalyptus Creek is going to make nonalcoholic wines,
Mitch. The patent is for a completely new process and
it works. No alcoholic residue at all and the taste! I
won't create any more Rafes."

"Babe, no—"

"My mind's made up. Finally. So don't try to change
it. You can't." She'd kissed his chin to mitigate the se-
verity of her tone.

"Hell." Mitch had raked his fingers through his hair.
"You're not the only one who's done some rethinking.
These past couple of years I've known your family . . . none of you uses booze as the easy road to obliv-
ion. It just sort of lubricates social occasions for you,
the same way you use hugging and laughter. It's part of
your tradition. I don't want to steal that from you."

Touched beyond words, Tish had pulled his hands
to her heart and held them there. Its quickened pulse
beat hard and fast against the skin roughened, she
knew, from gripping a gun. Tenderly she had lifted his
palms and kissed the calluses.

"It's the hugs and laughter that matter the most,
anyway," she'd pointed out.

"To jeopardize the success of your business—"

"I won't be doing that. Honestly. The market niche
for truly fine alcohol-free wine will be immense. Our
wine will be so hot it'll nuke the competition off the

shelves. We'll outsell bottled water. The cola companies will scream for mercy. Eucalyptus Creek is going to make a fortune." She laughed. "It's a good thing I've learned not to be corrupted by wealth because there's a distinct possibility the D'Angeli and Connor families are going to become stinking rich. Will that bug you?"

"What?"

"Being rich."

"I suppose I can handle it."

A long, satisfying kiss had followed.

Letizia's lips tingled from the memory. Pa gave her a surreptitious wink as he paced solemnly to her side, and offered his arm. Tish winked at him and smiled. The music crescendoed and they started walking down the aisle.

Nonna was in the front pew, looking at her. Beside her grandmother the governor smiled. More important to Letizia, Mitch's mother was sitting across the aisle, her expression peaceful. Other familiar faces blurred.

Only one figure stood out with real clarity: Mitch.

His warm gaze met hers as she approached. Letizia turned to Pa, raising her veil to accept his kiss on her cheek. She held her trailing bouquet of grape leaves wound through with stephanotis out to Belle—all without losing an instant of precious contact with the love in Mitch's eyes.

Trustingly, she put her hand in his.

To have and to hold, from this day forward. Cleaving only unto you. . . .

This month's
irresistible novels from

TEMPTATION

THE LAST HONEST MAN by Leandra Logan

Meet Jackson Monroe—another in Temptation's sinfully sexy line-up of men under the banner *Rebels & Rogues*. Jackson had returned to claim his wife, only to discover that stubborn Emaline had supposedly buried him six feet under. How was Jackson going to set things right?

MAN WITH A PAST by Jayne Ann Krentz

Cole Stockton was devastatingly sexy, or so Kelsey Murdock thought. But he was also a man of mystery—and that worried her. A relationship should be honest, open from the start, and he seemed to have something to hide. . .

CAPTIVATED by Carla Neggers

Who needed a man who oozed sensuality? To her annoyance Sheridan Weaver found out *she* did. Richard St. Charles, with his free and easy life-style, didn't fit into her routine. What would happen if she threw caution away?

UNDER HER INFLUENCE by Kelly Street

Mitch Connor believed in rules—professionally and personally. Which meant never getting involved with beautiful Tish D'Angeli. But after one sizzling kiss. . . he was breaking all the rules!

Spoil yourself next month
with these four novels from

TEMPTATION

THE WOLF by Madeline Harper

Meet Jake Forrester—another in Temptation's sinfully sexy
line-up of men under the banner *Rebels & Rogues*. As sheriff,
Jake ran *his* territory *his* way—until beautiful Julia Shelton
arrived and started stirring up trouble...

TALLAHASSEE LASSIE by Peg Sutherland

Playing Jammin' J.T., the outrageous disc jockey, was easy.
Being insecure Jillian Joyner was another matter. Especially
when Jillian discovered that her neighbour was Russ Flynn,
the DJ she had been hired to beat in the ratings!

ASK DR. KATE by Vicki Lewis Thompson

Garth Fredericks wasn't about to be taken in by a sex-starved
media broad...nor did he need to read her phenominally
successful "how to" sex manual. But faced with the real, soft,
vulnerable side of Dr. Kate, how could Garth prove to her that
he wasn't just another guy on the make?

THE RIGHT MOVES by Sharon Mayne

Adventure was Dusty Rose's middle name—as it was her
father's. So when he mysteriously disappeared in Arizona,
Dusty was hot on his trail. Then macho Miguel Santiago
insisted that she needed his help...

EXPERIENCE THE EXOTIC

VISIT . . . INDONESIA, TUNISIA, EGYPT AND MEXICO . . . THIS SUMMER

Enjoy the experience of exotic countries
with our Holiday Romance Pack

Four exciting new romances by favourite
Mills & Boon authors.

Available from July 1993   Price: £7.20

*Available from W.H. Smith, John Menzies, Martins, Forbuoys,
most supermarkets and other paperback stockists.
Also available from Mills & Boon Reader Service, FREEPOST,
PO Box 236, Thornton Road, Croydon, Surrey CR9 9EL.
(UK Postage & Packaging free)*